MW00532499

Those Who Went Remain There Still

Those Who Went Remain There Still

Cherie Priest

Subterranean Press 2008

Those Who Went Remain There Still

First Edition

ISBN
978-1-59606-179-8

Subterranean Press
PO Box 190106
Burton, MI 48519

www.subterraneanpress.com

This one's for
all my friends and family
in the Bluegrass State

No gypsy slut nor doxy,
shall win my Mad Tom from me
I'll weep all night, the stars I'll fight,
the fray shall well become me.

—from "Mad Maudlin's Search
for Her Tom of Bedlam"
Author unknown

Acknowledgements

Even the cheesiest little monster stories don't happen without help, and this one took a bundle. I'll start by thanking my darling husband Aric, who brings home the bacon and the health insurance so that I can stay home and write my cheesy little monster stories. Thanks also goes to Dear Mr. Schafer, who takes the most marvelous chances on newbies like me; to my agent Jennifer Jackson, who must be one of the busiest people alive (but she always has time for emailed questions and nervous phone calls); and to my sister, who does not yet know that she's going to get stuck helping me with the final pass proof edits for this manuscript. I'm not above bribing her if need be, and she's usually game to help give me a read, so I'm pretty confident that I won't feel silly about including this note once the book is actually in print.

Likewise, I extend my fondest thanks to Mike Owen and Laura Middleton, who took one for the team by investigating Rock City for me, in order to track down the source of this book's title. (It's kind of a long story.) Thanks also to Ron Nagy from the Lily Dale Assembly, who tried to help me prove that John Coy had lived in that town, once upon a time.

And strangely enough, a great deal of additional thanks goes to my mother, Sharon Priest. My mom is a generally helpful soul, so it's not strange that she would lend a hand, really—except that she hates scary stories and has never read a single one of mine. The odds are exceedingly good that she'll never read this one, either, but this did not prevent her from rummaging about through storage and digging up old genealogy records at my behest. She helped me confirm some of the historical specifics even though she knew exactly what I was going to do with them, and she'll probably be mortified by the final product. I greatly appreciate that, despite her reservations, she's been such a good sport about the whole thing.

So yes, in case you read this book but skip the accompanying chapbook, it's worth noting that this short novel is inspired by an old family tale which—sadly enough—features no actual monsters in its original incarnation. I assure you that this retelling rectifies reality's troubling oversight in this matter.

I.

In the Beginning: Reflections upon the Wilderness Road, Daniel Boone, 1775

WE'D BEEN CUTTING SINCE March, and we were almost done.

Back at the start, there were thirty-six of us. By fall, we were down to twenty-two men.

You could blame a couple of our losses on the Shawnee. Them and the Chickamaugas, they didn't agree to any Transylvania treaty, and they didn't think we belonged there. But we only lost two men to the natives and the rest of us kept on cutting. Then one man got taken by a bear, back in June. It was a big old momma, with a couple of round, fat babies. She got him good, but he ought to have known better.

Three more we lost just to being sick, or hurt, or working too hard. One of them, an axe-head came flying off a handle and notched his shoulder, and the wound didn't look too bad except how it wouldn't heal right. It was a real trouble, an accident like that, but it wasn't the kind of dying that scared men off a task.

It was the rest of them, the other eight. They were the ones we were scared about.

But we couldn't do anything except keep our eyes open and our axes swinging. We were almost to the Kentucky River, and it was stupid of me, maybe, but I thought if we could just get to the river, we'd be all right.

We'd brought that Road from Virginia to the middle of Kentucky, almost 200 miles. We blazed that Road up through the Cumberland Gap just like I said we would, and I promised we'd clean it up until we got into the thick of the new territory.

Well, we sure got into the thick of *something*.

I just kept on thinking about the river, and I kept thinking about the flying thing, and the way it swayed and waddled up there between the treetops. It was heavy—too heavy to fly, almost. It was all the creature could do to hop and flap between the branches.

I kept thinking, *If we can just get ourselves across that river, it'll be wide enough that once we cross, the thing won't be able to follow us.* Maybe I was just saying that because it gave us a goal, and it made the men feel like there was a safe place ahead. I hoped I wasn't lying to them.

But I'd seen a lot of strange things out there, out where nobody walks but the Indians in their deerskin moccasins. I'd seen cats the size of ponies, almost; and I'd seen bears with chests like barrels, and heads like a moon's eclipse.

For all my time out in the trees, and for all the years I spent watching, hunting, and taming the wild spots between the little cities…I'd never seen anything like *that*.

To tell it true, for a long time we could hardly see it at all.

The creature mostly came at night, and at first, it mostly came for the food we'd caught and were keeping. We figured it must be coyotes. Wolves will catch and kill their own food, but a coyote isn't above stealing it. They're lazy things, and sneaky and fast. But we weren't hurting for food, and we found it aggravating, not frightening.

It was strange, though, about the food. Coyotes will take your store, but they won't foul what they leave. They might come back and take the rest later, but they don't shit on it out of spite.

When the trouble began in earnest, it was still late summer, or the very earliest fall. Mostly it was plenty hot, and we ought to have found lots of game. Up until fall we shot long-legged, fawn-gray deer and heavy little turkeys. We found plenty of nuts and bushels of berries.

But it got harder and harder to hunt down meat. All the game went wandering off, getting scarce. We had to travel farther and farther away from the Road in order to find anything at all; it was like the whole forest knew there was danger, and it wasn't just a few dozen men clearing a path.

We were armed, all of us.

We each had a sharp axe, at least—and some of us had guns and arrows, too. We weren't homesteaders, waiting helpless. We came ready for trouble, and ready to hand out trouble.

But we had *no idea*—none at all—and it got worse every day. We only got hungrier, and more nervous as the weeks ticked by and we worked hard, sunup to sundown, and there were shadows covering the stars. Terrible smells came pouring through the camp like the stench of death itself, and all night we heard the sound of wings bigger than wagon wheels, flapping up above like the snap and unsnap of an umbrella.

The first man went missing all of a sudden, and after that the creature took somebody almost every other night. Towards the end it slowed down some, going two or even three nights without stealing anyone. We must've been getting harder to grab. That thing pared us down to the fastest, and the hardest to hold.

Those of us who remained were going to give it one hell of a fight, if that's what it wanted.

But the first one, he didn't know. None of us knew, and we weren't even sure what happened. All we knew was that it was dark and he was screaming, and along with his screaming we heard something else. It was a louder noise than a man could've made. It came from a bigger chest, a raspy honking, something like a goose—and something like the shriek of a big cat. If you've ever heard one of those cats, you know what I mean. They sound like a woman, almost, like she's screaming for help. It's a noise that'll make your blood run cool, and make you sweat at the same time. Imagine that cry, if you can, and imagine it with a croak.

I'm not saying what I mean too well.

Anyway, he was taken and we were suddenly short another warm body, and we didn't like that too much. But we kept cutting. Deep down we knew it wasn't a cat, and it wasn't a wolf, either. Any fool knows the sound of a wolf. Even people who've never heard it before, they'll recognize the howl and run away from it, if they've got any sense.

We talked about how it might be a bear, but bears just roar and that's a sound we all knew. So it wasn't a bear, either.

It was about as big as one, though, and it moved above us, and not beside us. We'd been learning, by trial and error, by glimpse and fast-moving wink between the trees.

Whatever it was, it was flesh and blood, and feathers too. We found the feathers sometimes in the morning—huge brown things tipped with gray and a rubbed copper color. Someone said that it must be an owl, and if we hadn't been so tired, hungry, and mad, we would've laughed at him.

I'd seen owls the size of dogs, and I'd seen turkeys even bigger than that. But none of them leaves feathers as long as a small canoe, or as wide as a fat man's leg. No, our visitor was bigger than I was. It was bigger even than Little Heaster, who we called "little" because it was funny. That boy wasn't eighteen yet, but he was a head and a half bigger than the rest of us.

The creature was stronger than we were too, and it must've seen real good in the dark. Maybe light hurt its eyes. Anyway, it didn't like the fire. That's why we built it up so big at night. We thought maybe if camp was bright enough and hot enough, we'd keep the thing away.

See, it's never been the axes that separate us from the beasts. It's not steel, and not tools, and not roads. It's the fire, that's all. Everything under creation—everything on four legs and everything that swims or flies or crawls—every living thing except for a man will shy far from a flame.

And night kept falling fast. It fell faster every dusk, or we were losing more of our daylight gathering and hacking up fuel to burn.

Come night, the birds quit calling and the squirrels, porcupines, and lizards all quit their scurrying. Nothing moved beneath the leaves on the floor between the tree trunks. Nothing crawled across the boulders pushed down the hills by the gullywashing rains.

The sky went orange, then lilac. Then it went gray and took on a touch of blue.

Those nights, I would've been happy to hear the howling chatter of a pack of wolves. Those nights it would've warmed my heart to hear that lady-fierce scream that says a mountain lion is hungry nearby.

We made a fire so bright we couldn't see the moon. We had our steel and we had arms so used to swinging, we could snap down oaks in our sleep. Between us, we could keep away a cat or a whole crowd of dogs.

We all huddled close to the edges of the fire—so close that we almost got burned, and we were so hot we could barely stand it.

Not far away, not nearly far enough away, we caught a loud series of pops.

It was a strange sound, and when it came we heard the high-up branches crack and fall. The pops were harsh and hollow, and they climbed through the sky like wings lifted up by the beating of a drum.

Over and over again, it was the fast, low snap you hear when a strong-armed woman throws open a wet blanket.

II.

Ames, Iowa—1899

I was eighteen when I left Leitchfield, and I had my reasons. I had them by the bushel.

Same as everyone else I was born there, at home. And same as everyone else I was brought up confused, and hateful in a way. It could be that we're just a fractious lot, as old Heaster Jr. used to say. Maybe we were all born ready to squabble and we wouldn't have liked one another anyhow, but most people blamed the feuding on the war.

You had to blame it on something, if you weren't going to blame it on yourself.

The way things split up was like this: Heaster Jr. was the great granddaddy of us all—either by blood or by marriage. And by blood or by marriage, most of his offspring (leastways, most of us who stayed in the valley) had wound up wearing one of two last names, Coy or Mander.

When the war broke out and Kentucky was asked to choose sides, we went both ways on both sides of the church rows, but it mostly broke down by family lines. The Manders sent eleven sons, brothers, and cousins up to the Union. They got seven of them back. The Coys sent thirteen sons, brothers, and cousins to the Confederacy. They got back four.

One of the ones who came back was my daddy, Everett Coy. He married Mona Manny in 1870 and I happened along nine months and three days after. They named me Meshack, and I didn't know until I was a grown man how they'd spelled it wrong. Momma said she'd heard it in church and thought it sounded nice. Daddy never said anything about it, 'cause he died when he got kicked in the head by a horse, and I was just ten. Neither one of them, Momma or Daddy, could read or write hardly, and I don't hold that against them and I'm not saying they were stupid. I'm just saying there was no one there to teach them, so they didn't know.

That's how it worked there, in the bluegrass hills. You learned how to live close to the land because you weren't close to much else.

There weren't many people except those you were related to, and probably fighting with. There weren't many towns closer than several days away, and once you got there you'd need money to do anything.

Well, we didn't have any money. So we made just about everything for ourselves. Oh, sometimes we traded for something—mostly we swapped homebrewed alcohol for staples like cloth, nails, and seed. But mostly, if we couldn't make it ourselves we went without it.

That went for books, same as the rest of it. We only had one school, and it wasn't open half the year, and sometimes it wasn't open that much—depending on the teacher. Our preacher could read, and if you gave him the right kind of moonshine he might teach you a few letters, but he was a cold old fellow who shouted at us about love. He beat us with words of kindness. He kicked us with commands that we should be gentle and patient.

Most of us didn't like him much. But my momma would go, every Sunday. She would sit there with my little sister, Winnter, and they would rest themselves on those wood-slat pews so hard you could've cracked nuts on them. I don't know what they learned there, that they liked it enough to go back every week. By the time I was old enough to listen good, I was old enough to work—so I worked, and I didn't get any other education until I left.

I would've left when Daddy died, if I'd been able. Momma told me then how I was the man of the house, me being oldest. She explained how I had new responsibilities, with her getting old and a baby sister to love after. Momma wasn't twenty-five when that happened.

She was younger then than I was when I went back.

I'd like to tell you how that gives me some perspective, and how I'm more understanding about why she did the things she did, but that'd be a lie. I understood well enough then that she was crazy, and I could see in Winnter—in the way her eyes went wild sometimes, and the way she would laugh and cry or hug or hit for no real reason—I could see something mad was in the family. And I spent half my life praying, "Not me, too. Whatever it was, don't let me have caught it too."

For a long time, I thought there might be hope for Winnter. I thought if nothing else, maybe she'd marry good. She was real pretty, with hair that copper-brown color you see on birds, and those eyes that were blue and speckled gold. She was too thin, but we were all too thin from not eating right, or enough. She couldn't read or write, but most of us couldn't either, so it weren't no strike against her.

But she could make a rhubarb pie that would make Jesus himself crawl down from the cross to lick his fingers. And she could sew real fine—she could mend up anything, and if there was cloth enough, she could make up her own dresses and they were as good as anything you'd see in a city catalog.

And like I said, she was awful pretty.

It didn't matter, though. The older she got the more she behaved like Momma. I tried to guide her some, because she was my responsibility and because I loved her. I wanted her to understand that just because she lived with Momma, and just because she looked like her, she didn't have to *be* her. She didn't have to turn into the lonely, crazy old spinster who hates the whole world—Mander, Coy, and everybody else, too. I tried to tell her there were other places and other families, other spots where she could go and get more for herself.

I told her, "There's a whole world outside of Leitchfield. There's a whole bunch of other states, outside of Kentucky. There's a whole bunch of other people you could grow up and marry, and not a one of them has to be from anyplace you've ever heard of."

But she turned farther and farther inward. She wandered around by herself a lot, and she quit talking much to anyone except Momma. As Winnter got older she and Momma started to fight more and more, and that was the toughest thing to watch because I couldn't interfere and if I got between them, they'd both turn on me.

They were too much alike, that's what everybody said. Two cats in a wet sack, the pair of them.

And then, Winnter left.

It didn't surprise me as much as it should have, but usually when she talked she was just talking, and she didn't mean anything. She made threats and promises like little prayers, and eventually no one listened—not even me. I shouldn't say I didn't care anymore, because I did care. But I do have to say that I'd quit listening.

She said, "It's calling me again," and I gave her the same warning I always gave. She probably knew it by heart.

I said, "Nothing's calling you, Winnter. Nothing's waiting for you out there in that cave."

She didn't look at me, because she didn't need to. She had her answer handy. "Why, because it's not far enough away?"

It was no secret, how I wanted to leave. It was no secret either, how far I meant to go. So I told her, "If you just give me another year, I'll take you out of here with me. We can start someplace else. You can marry someone you've never seen before, since you don't like the look of anyone you know."

"And you can do the same?" I'm telling you, she wasn't dumb.

"Sure, I'd like to do the same," I admitted. "There's nothing here I want, and nothing here that's good. It's just a place to stay ignorant and work hard and starve. And I'm sick of it."

"You don't know where you'll go, do you?"

"Haven't made up my mind."

Winnter turned to me then, and stared at me hard—in that way where I swear, she saw right past me and was watching something else. "That's 'cause whatever's calling you, it's so far away you can hardly hear it. This isn't like that, not for me. I hear it clear, because it's close. I'm going to leave this place as sure as you will, but I'm not going with you, and I'm not going far."

Then she turned and walked off, back into the crackerbox house with the floors that creaked if you breathed on them.

Two days later, she hiked out to Heaster Junior's back acres and vanished inside the old cave we all called the Witch's Pit. Best as anyone knows, she died there. But no one ever found her. No one ever went very far to look for her though. And that's not an accusation. I'm not blaming anybody.

I didn't go in there either. As far as we knew, she was the only one who ever did.

Anyway, once she was gone it was just me and Momma. That arrangement lasted all of a week before I ran off too.

I didn't have any money, but I didn't have anything else holding me there in that miserable place, that poor, furious place where everyone's angry at everyone else, and no one feels like anyone can get away. Maybe that's why they're all so mad—Mander, Coy, and everyone else. Everybody just feels trapped.

It's no excuse, I don't think. You don't shoot each other and swear at each other and steal each other's property for a reason like that. If you're all that unhappy, buck up and leave. I did it, and I was hardly more than a boy. It wasn't easy, and I'm not saying it was;

but it was easier than living that way—stuck and surrounded in a blighted valley filled with enemies.

I packed up what little I owned and I hiked up north to Louisville. I hopped a train, at first hiding like a stowaway, and later working my way along the lines by shoveling coal and unloading freight.

So it was north, first. For awhile I worked in Chicago. And then I went west, and I finally ran out of steam in Iowa. There, I worked on another man's farm for a couple of years…and in time, I scraped up enough money for a home of my own and a wife of my own.

I married Sarah and we made a place together. We made four children together too, in just six years—and there was a fifth to come that day when I opened my front door, there in Ames, Iowa, on property that belonged to me and no other man. We were three months short of another peaceful Coy being born into a land of hard work and reward, not angry relatives who killed one another over scraps.

We were only weeks away from another welcome addition, not another unplanned burden, when I found Titus Mander standing on my stoop with his hat in his hands.

We just looked at each other for a few seconds. It took me that long to recognize him.

By then, it'd been ten years since I'd seen him and he was grown up like I was. Two men, not two boys who'd once tried to strangle each other over an apple. He stood quiet-like and patient on my porch. I had a field behind him, and it was almost ready for harvesting so the corn was high and bright, beautiful green. The pale, butter-white tops of silk swayed in the wind, and Titus held himself real still and let me look at him.

He looked different. His hair was darker. He wasn't all skin and bones like last time I'd seen him, and he was wearing clothes that were plain, but clean. He'd gotten taller, but he still wasn't as tall as me.

"Titus." I said, and it wasn't a question—except for how I wondered what he was doing there. I knew who he was.

"Meshack." He knew who I was, too. Of course he did. He'd come looking for me, or that's what I had to figure.

"What are you doing here, Titus?" I used his name again because it made me feel more like I was in control, which was silly. We were on my property, on my own land that I worked with my own two hands. This was my house, my front stair—and behind me I had my wife, and my children. I don't know why the very sight of him made me so nervous. He wasn't armed that I could see, and he didn't look like he was angry about anything.

He twisted the brim of a hat in his hands. "Meshack, I'm not here for trouble," he said, like he knew he needed to assure me. It must be true what they say about old habits and how hard they are to lay aside. But I appreciated how hard he was trying, so I was willing to try too.

"If you don't bring any, there won't be any," I told him, and I meant it.

He exhaled. "That's fair," he said. "And that's part of why I'm here. Things might be changing."

"How's that?"

"Well, it took him almost a whole century to do it, but Heaster Wharton Junior's finally died. If he split all that property up right, then everything might settle down, but there's something funny with the will."

I scratched at the side of my head and wrestled with whether or not I should invite him inside. "I don't understand. Why would news like that bring you all the way out here, to me?"

"Because your momma's named in the papers, but since she's gone, that means some of Heaster's leavings might go to you. At least, you need to be there while we sort it all out."

"She's gone?" I hadn't known.

"I'm sorry," he said, and the words made him uncomfortable. He shifted on his feet and pinched harder at his hat. "I didn't mean to break it to you. I figured you'd heard."

"I hadn't," I said. "How'd she go?"

"Don't know. I heard they just found her in that old house you used to live in, and she'd been gone awhile. Maybe she'd been sick.

But it was a couple of years ago. And they didn't call you home for it?"

"Nobody sent for me." I wasn't sure what to say, because I wasn't sure how I felt. I was trying to sort it out while I was standing there talking to him. Was I sad about it? Angry that no one'd told me? None of that sounded right.

"I'm sorry," he said again.

"It's no fault of yours."

He loosened his grip on his hat and said, "I appreciate you saying so. Listen, there's a train leaving in the morning. I'm going to be on it, and I'm here inviting you to come with me. Things are different now, for some of us. After you left, some of the rest of us took off too. I was one of them. I got out. And now I've got to go home, and I think you've got to go home too."

I leaned against the doorframe, still trying to tell myself I didn't really feel relieved to know my mother had been called home to Jesus, or to whoever else would have her. But I couldn't convince myself, and I was leaving a man standing on my porch, wondering if I was going to punch him or invite him in for supper.

"Well then," I said, standing back a foot or two and giving him room. "I guess you'd better come on inside."

III.

Lily Dale, NY—1899

It was an anniversary of sorts. Twenty years ago we founded this great experiment, and my, how it had grown. Our community blossomed so beautifully. Our ranks had swollen. Our town increased in wisdom and stature, and our reputation for education and spiritual assistance reached around the world, and back.

As I strolled down those prettily trimmed streets with their electrically lit walkways, I was proud—very proud—to have been part of its making. We built up lovely, warm, and comfortable homes for ourselves and our visitors. We advertised the means in which we wished to help; every street pointed to a medium, to an advisor, to a specialist in the cards or healing.

I tapped my cane along the white railed fences as I walked. I waved and smiled at my neighbors, and I looked forward to the summer camp meetings. We could expect guests by the thousands.

I could not help but smile, and I thought, "Truly this is a great land, where the old ways of superstition and religious intolerance can be shunted aside, and room can be made for the evolution of belief. Truly the way we pray is a science, too, and it ought to be investigated as such. For there is a heaven above us, and it is bustling with life, although we here below might not know it while we wear these mortal shells."

My mood was light and the day was fine when I returned to my own cottage and I found the mail had been delivered. I looked in the box from habit more than expectation. But on that day, I had a letter.

The postmark nearly stopped my heart.

I jerked the envelope up to my face and examined it closely, distracting myself—delaying myself from opening it. I investigated it like a policeman. Did I know this handwriting? What kind of paper was it? Who could have written it?

There was no name on the left, but in the middle my name was composed in precise, tight letters—so it wasn't written by any near relation of mine. Bless them, even the ones who can read a little can scarcely print at all.

John Coy
Cassadega Way
Lily Dale, NY

And it had come from Lexington. *Not Leitchfield*, I told myself, but it was a small and false comfort. Lexington was the next nearest town of any size, and if any official business needed attending, it would surely take place there.

I was still standing beside the box, outside my door.

I let myself in and set my cane on a side table. I clutched the letter and still, I refused to open it. I turned it over and over between my fingers, hunting for clues that might tell me the contents would not break my heart, or horrify me, or terrify me, or—worst of all—summon me home.

In the corner beside the fireplace, I had placed a large rocker chair. I dropped myself down into it and ran my fingers over the letter. Of course it would summon me home. No lesser mission would require such correspondence. No other task would require any communication, not after so many years.

And how many years? I considered the question and had to think. I had to calculate it, how many years had I been gone before I came to help make Lily Dale? Only a few, I believed. For the sake of settling my own nerves and letting the query drop, I concluded that it must have been five or more, and twenty-five years in total was a solid amount. The realization hit me hard. It pressed against my chest so heavily that I closed my eyes. I let the envelope fall into my lap, where it rested on top of my legs.

It had been a quarter of a century since I'd left Leitchfield, Kentucky.

By the time I received that letter, I had lived longer outside of the valley than I'd lived within it, though that margin was slim.

When I'd escaped, yes—that's what it was.

It *was* an escape, and for years I thought of myself as a refugee. When I escaped I was a young man but a grown man, and a suspect man because I hadn't yet married. It didn't matter what they thought of me; at least, it didn't matter once I became tall enough and tough enough to deter the criticisms and assaults of my brothers.

They hated me because I liked to read, and they could not even sign their own names, except for an x-shaped mark. They worried for the family's status when I didn't want any of the scraggly, illiterate women they pushed upon me. They attacked me for wanting more, and they burned the books I scraped to steal or buy.

What an accusation it is, too, that a boy could "live above his raisin'," as if anyone should aspire to less.

They meant it as an insult but I refused to hear it that way. I heard their threats as a horse hears the lash of a crop. Let them swing, and let them shout. I don't know if they meant to push me as hard or as far as they did, but their efforts did more to send me away than any mere encouragement might have.

I went to Boonesborough, and I stole what I needed or I begged for it. And I got lucky, after a few months. There was a teacher who traveled from town to town, showing children how to count or spell. He said that if I'd carry his things and work for him, he'd feed me and put me up. And he did, as far as Louisville. I left him there because I couldn't stand him, the filthy drunk, and by then I could read and write well enough to find a better position with a shipping company.

At that firm, I watched the figures and marked down shipments in the great leather ledger we restocked with sheets of paper as big as pillowcases. I wasn't very good at the numbers, but I was better than the man who owned the operation and besides, if I'd been any more professional they would've had to pay me more.

Sometimes I wrote out letters for other people, letters that would be carried on the riverboats that steamed back and forth along the Ohio. I made extra change that way, listening to men and women who'd never learned or never took to learning.

I thought, "This is what it must be like to be a priest."

They told you everything, those people did. Who was alive, who was dying, and who got married because they had to. I heard it all, and I took my task seriously. They trusted me to transcribe and forget. I did my best to fulfill that obligation with integrity.

And then, one day, I took a letter that would change my life.

There was a woman, small and plain, quiet and intelligent looking.

When she spoke, her voice was lower than I'd expected. She explained that she needed to send a message down to Atlanta, to her parents there. She warned me that it might take a long time to write, because she had much to say—but she'd brought her own paper and she was prepared to pay whatever fees I required.

And the story she told…the tale she laid out for her family back in Georgia…

It was a tale of two sisters, and of hope beyond the grave. It was her testimonial of faith, and it was her declaration of independence.

She spoke up and I wrote down. I tried not to interrupt her with questions but it was difficult. This woman, her name was Patricia, she had a wonderful way of telling stories. I remember that we sat together near the river, in the shadow of the bridge behind us. I remember how the sun was working its way through my shirt and underneath the rim of my hat, and I was growing so warm that I feared I might faint.

But she kept talking, and I kept writing.

I won't say that Patricia converted me. She transformed me. She opened my eyes to things I'd never before imagined. Listening to that tiny, lovely woman speak I could almost believe that everything in my life—every miserable moment when I was brought up slowly, and in darkness—it all was leading to a reasonable, joyful meeting with this petite saint with her ash-gold hair and her lavender dress.

In her final paragraph she declared that she was going north, and that she would not be returning south of the Ohio River, not at any point and not for any reason.

I finally interrupted her then. I was unable to prevent myself. I told her, "You are the bravest woman I've ever met." And she smiled, and she invited me to come with her.

"We've begun to fashion our own communities," she said. "There's talk of a town—can you believe that? A whole town made of devout, brilliant people who commune with the spirits. There are more like me. And we'll need more men like you, educated men with eager spirits and curious minds, not to mention strong backs for building. Have you ever done any carpentry?"

"Sure," I said, because it was just one of those things you learned in the hills. Even if you didn't do it well, you could saw a board in two or nail two boards into one.

"If you're serious, you can follow me up. I'm traveling with two other girls, and we could use a man alongside us. Sometimes it's hard for women to go alone. Sometimes people want to stop us, or change our minds and send us home to our fathers or husbands."

I glanced down at her hand and saw no ring. If she noticed that I'd looked, she didn't say anything.

"It's wrong, for the world to work like that, but I know the way things are," she said. "I believe—I really do believe—that if everyone knew what was waiting for us on the other side…if everyone understood how this life, it's only the beginning, then things would change. I think men and women might treat each other differently, or better. And this wonderful new church could be the key. So many of the mediums who speak so clearly to the other side—so many of them are women."

"Are you a medium?" I asked, because it interested me greatly.

"No," she said. "But my sister has a great gift. I've seen what she can do, and I have something stronger than faith. I have certainty in a soul that lasts longer than our short span of mortal years. I have pure and perfect knowledge that life continues. It surpasses the grave. It lingers, and we linger. The dead who left before us linger, and if we are prepared to listen, they are prepared to speak. So will you, John? Will you come up with us?"

"Yes," I told her, breathless with excitement at the prospect. "Yes, I will come with you. Let me come with you. Let me help."

The letter was still on my lap, the one I'd received from Kentucky. I didn't want to touch it. I didn't want to open it. I didn't want to know what it said inside, but that eager and curious nature of mine wouldn't let me tear it to shreds, either, although I considered it.

I held it up between two thumbs and two fingers, and I flexed my wrists as if to rip the thing into pieces.

And there was a knock on my door.

Shirley announced herself and came inside. Older than me by ten years and beginning to shrink, I think. Shirley was Patricia's sister. She was one of the women I'd escorted up the river, and then up the continent those decades ago.

"I hope I'm not interrupting," she said, and her face froze with concern. "Is something wrong?"

"No," I said too quickly.

"Liar," she said right back.

"You're right, I'm lying. But it's not a deliberate deception I'm only..." I held the letter out to her and begged with my eyes. "Afraid."

"What's this, then?" she asked, and she took the envelope and held it to the light. Her eyes were beginning to fail her more each year, and they'd never been too strong in the first place.

"It arrived today."

"From Kentucky?" She squinted at the postmark.

"From Kentucky."

"And you haven't opened it."

"No. I told you. I'm afraid. I don't want to know what's inside," I half-lied again.

"If that were true, you would have torn it up already."

"But it might be important," I said weakly. "It must be important, if they sent it from Lexington. Someone went all the way to the city to have this sent, and I'll tell you the truth, I'm not certain how they found me. It makes me nervous that they know where to look."

"This 'they' you keep suggesting—do you mean your family?"

I nodded, slow with a valiant effort not to appear shameful. "My family. Or what's left of it."

Then her expression clouded. Her eyes flickered in a way I'd come to recognize. I straightened in my chair and resisted the impulse to reach again for the envelope.

"Someone's died," she said.

"I've assumed, but I can't imagine who it might be—that anyone would contact me about it."

"Not a parent."

"My parents have been dead since—"

"It wasn't a question," she chided me. "It's not a parent. It's an older man, a very old man. No one you ever loved. And..." She curled her fingers around the edge of the envelope. I wanted to tell her not to crease it, but I knew better so I didn't speak except to prompt her.

"And?"

She crushed her eyes closed and held the paper up against her breast. For a moment she looked stricken. When she spoke again, there was fear in her voice. "And perhaps you ought to tear it up, after all."

"I'm sorry?"

Shirley returned the envelope to me. I held it up, trying to see through the outer layer to get a better hint of what waited within.

"I don't like this," she said. "It's a summons from a dead man, and he's a hateful old thing. I can't see him and I can't reach him, not yet. He hasn't been gone long enough to interrogate. But the spirits are sending me warnings, serious warnings. Oh John, whatever he wants, don't give it to him!"

I was stunned by her spontaneous conviction. "What are you hearing, Shirley? What are you seeing?"

"Darkness. A world wet and black, without any light. And it is... and there is...madness." She cocked her head and said, not to me but to someone I couldn't see, "All right, I'll tell him. They say you shouldn't go. You're being invited home, but you shouldn't go. But they think you *will* go, anyway."

I held the envelope and slipped my fingernail under its seal. If I didn't open it soon, I wouldn't be able to do it at all. "As usual, they're probably right."

"John," she said, but she didn't say anything else.

The paper tore and the letter within crinkled as I pulled it out.

My eyes sped across the sheet and snagged on the important phrases. I said them aloud as I read them. "Williams and Katz, Attorneys at Law...last will and testament...property west of Leitchfield...conflict resolution..." My voice trailed off and Shirley was not very patient.

"What does it mean?" she demanded sweetly.

"Heaster Wharton Junior. He's finally dead. And you're right. I have to go home, just this one more time."

Shirley was listening to someone, and it wasn't me. "Yes," she said after a few seconds. "This *will* be the last time."

I felt cold, even though the day was warm and I was dressed almost too heavily for it. “But I have to go. It’s hard to explain.”

“I know,” she said, and she put her hand on my arm. “But it won’t be easy, and I’m afraid for you. The spirits don’t like this, but they want me to tell you—they’ll help you, if they can.”

IV.

The Mother: Reflections from the Road, Daniel Boone, 1775

WE CAME TO THINK of the flying, flapping thing as a "she."

There was something about the way she moved, like she was heavy and expecting. For a long time, we didn't ever see her too close, at least no one who survived had seen her up near. But even at a distance there was something womanly about the sway of her body, moving like a pendulum between her wings.

A mother bear, a mother lion. A mother wolf. She was angry and dangerous like they are, and like nothing else on earth.

I mean, God Himself knows you can make a male thing mad. You can wind him up and he'll see red, and he'll come for you, and he'll mean to tear you apart when he catches you. But that's nothing like the wrath of a mother when you stand between her and the thing she nurses.

I swear by all my upbringing, and by my own mother. I swear by my own wife, mother of my own young, and I swear by everything I ever learned about heaven: *I do not know what we ever did to rile her.*

All I could figure is there must've been a nest someplace, and we must have stumbled through it. But if that's how it went, why did she try so hard to keep us? Why wouldn't she let us move on? We would've been more than happy to leave her be, if we'd just known how. But she chased us, she harried us. During the day we shuffled ahead of her, chopping down a swath because that was our job and we were so close—if we didn't finish then, someone else would have to come behind us, and I never left anything unfinished.

No one cleaned up after me and no one ever had to finish up any job of mine.

The rest of the men agreed. Most of them were Scots-Irish, and before they came to the colonies they spent their lives fighting hard for a place in Ulster, and they didn't run from anything any sooner than I did.

We were scared and we were mad, but we were not getting run off, no matter what that crazy creature did. We hardly had three miles left. We could do it. We could finish it.

But she was making us think again about *how* we were going to do it.

One night, she came down hard—right up close to the fire. That's how we all got our first almost-good look at her, and saw her shape. The details were fuzzy, but that's how it is when you're in danger. Your body moves before your eyes have time to tell you what the trouble's about.

It started the same as always. She waited until it was getting late enough that half of us had nodded off, and the watch-keeping half was tired from staring. It hurts your eyes, after awhile—peering into blackness that doesn't move and doesn't brighten. It hurts them just as bad as if you stared into the flames for hours.

And then, the fellows who were awake said it got real quiet, like when there's a cat or a wolf. They turned their faces to the treetops above us, and they waited to hear those first cracks of something heavy settling down, and pushing up, and taking wing.

They didn't have long to wait. She was coming, from not too far away.

Most of us woke up when the first loud snap happened. Me and these fellows had all been logging before, and when the big branches fall but you're underneath them, and there's no time to move—they call those limbs the widowmakers. So you hear that crack, loud as half a tree coming down, and a lot of these men knew to jump right up. They were ready to move before they were even awake.

We all stood there, running our hands along our axe-handles and panting, like sleeping had been real hard work and we'd just stopped it long enough to see what was going on.

Nothing happened, not for a few minutes. Wherever she was, she kept bouncing around up high, tree to tree, breaking branches and flapping those huge, horrible wings. Sometimes she'd make that cry, too—half honk, half scream. It wasn't a warning. It was a threat.

But none of her threats made sense. They never did. If she wanted us to leave, she sure wasn't making it easy for us. If she wanted us to leave her alone, she needed to quit attacking us.

It must've been something else, then, more like a war whoop. She didn't want to chase us off, she wanted to kill us all.

Little Heaster told me he thought maybe she's hungry, and that's all it is. I didn't know if that should make us feel better or worse about it.

That cry came up closer on us, and real fast, real sudden. She'd been out a ways, and then she was right on top of us. She moved over us like a shot. She bounded around between the branches, dipping down low—and when she swung close, that scream was enough to break your ears.

When she landed, near above us but high, a massive spray of leaves doused us all. And we shuddered and shook them off, and we realized that it wasn't leaves alone that hit us—the damn thing

M. Geyer

was pissing on us, too. Her piss was milky and it smelled rancid. She must have a bladder like a salt pork barrel, because she drenched a couple of the fellows in such a way that they were soaked just about to the bone.

There was a great outcry from our camp, and a couple of men fired shots into the air, trying to score a hit right up her underside to pay her back.

Something must've hit, because she squawked and beat her big old wings so hard it felt like a storm; but she did herself wrong when she thrashed around so hard. The force of her feathers fanned our fire like crazy, scattering a few small logs and bright sparked shards of kindling. We ran around kicking at them with our boots, knocking them back into the cleared spot for the dirt. It wouldn't do anyone any good for us to burn the whole forest down.

Mind you, I thought about letting the bright sticks smolder—just for a minute there. I don't mean to tell you we were getting desperate, but we were thinking about all our options. She took us, one after the other like she was plucking eggs out from under a hen. She swooped up to the trees with the bodies of my men, and she tore them up so we were splashed in their blood, and her piss, and the spittle she flung while she brought her face through their ribs and into their hearts.

And I didn't mean it, not really, but I mumbled and maybe Little Heaster heard me. I said, "We ought to let it catch, and clear the trees the faster way. Let her hide from us then."

Little Heaster gave me a look and I shook my head. "No. I'm just talking to hear myself. Help me catch these things and push them back. We don't really want to burn Kentucky down. We're not finished cutting through it yet."

The boy nodded and cringed when the shrieking squawk pierced the campsite again, but he charged after the nearest rolling log of fire and ash, and with the back of his axe's head he tapped it back over to the fire pit. The log rolled as clean as a croquet ball and stopped, and I told him it was a good job.

He's a good lad, but I wondered if I ought to have brought him. He was awful young for work like that; and yes he was bigger than the rest of us, and yes he had arms that could crush a bull's ribs, but he was still just a boy. He'd been keeping close to me since things got strange, and I hadn't said a thing about it.

All of them were my responsibility, and I meant to keep them all safe if I could. But I especially felt the need to look out for that one, who was the same age as one of mine back home.

While her wings beat she was cawing, and kicking, and bark shreddings were raining down with leaves but at least her bladder was empty and those of us who dodged fast enough the first time were staying dry.

And after a few seconds she was gagging. It sounded exactly like a cat my wife kept, a big orange Tom who's a better mouser than any trap I ever heard of. But that noise, it sounded like a bird the size of a bear trying to hock up a cat's ball of fur. We all cringed and we wanted to run off but there was nothing we could do except hang close at the fire's edge and kick back all the little coals that were scattering, rolling, falling away from the pit with the force of the wind she gusted up with her wings.

And then, dear God above, she coughed a wet, jumbled-up pile of bones and gristle and hair right down into the middle of us.

It plopped down on the edge of the fire, and where it landed the flames licked it and it sizzled.

Maybe the thing above us was resting. Maybe it tired her out to throw up something so huge, and it *was* huge—roughly the size and shape of what's left over when you gut a big deer. Anyway, she quit her flapping and quit her shrieking, but she didn't leave. She was still hanging up there, hulking her big, ugly body on whatever branch was strong enough to hold her.

It was like she was waiting for us to investigate. She wanted us to take a look at it. She wanted us to see what she'd done.

And it was right there, lying by the fire so we could see it just fine.

I pointed my finger around at my men all slow-like, so they knew I was pointing at all of them. And I said, "Everyone hold your axes or your guns right and ready. And keep looking up, I don't care what she throws up or pisses down. You watch for her."

And I crept between them, my own axe in my hand, but I held it down and low. When I got to the mess on the ground, I used the axe head to nudge it out of the ashes a little bit, because it was getting black and dampening the flames.

Mostly the steel head pushed at the mass and dented it, like pushing a spoon against thick pudding, or gravy that's gone too cold to pour. But then I heard a little knock—a sharp sound that told me this wasn't all hair and wet. That's when the skull toppled out, round and eaten clean until it was perfectly white.

I looked closer.

And I saw cloth with stitching on it still, even where the creature's stomach juice had eaten it into rags. At the top of the pile, tied and tangled into slimy brown knots, were a pair of leather bootlaces.

Here and there ribs poked up through the mess, and here and there were little pebble-like bones from toes or fingers; and I could make out a handful of teeth. I tapped them with the edge of my axe, and they crumbled away from the jawbone that held them.

I was so mad I could hardly see straight. I could hardly hold my axe without shaking the head right off the handle.

But I didn't have time to stay mad. I think she was watching me sort through that clump of leftovers she'd spit down into our camp. I think she was waiting for me to figure out how she'd savored what she wanted and threw out the rest, just like an owl does when it's finished with a meal.

Again I remembered making fun of someone for saying it was an owl.

And now I wondered if maybe I hadn't been wrong to laugh so fast.

She wasn't any owl like anything I'd ever shot, seen, or heard about, but maybe that was as close as we were going to guess it without bringing her down and taking her apart for ourselves.

But once I stood up straight, wondering what I was going to do with what was left of whoever it was she'd coughed up, she gave a big lunge—we heard it, the bough she was perched on snapped and broke, and fell—and she lifted herself up into the night.

V.

The Trip and the Task

Titus and I left first thing, next morning. My wife didn't like it any, but she understood and I kissed her good-bye with a promise I'd be home in a few weeks. That was all she asked, really. She wanted me to be home before the next baby came.

In some respects, it was much easier going from east to west. That's the way the world expects you to go—following gold, or land, or whatever other opportunity you see fit to chase. But getting back to Kentucky from Iowa was a hop, skip, and jump affair of trains, carts, and borrowed horses. It felt like swimming upstream.

On the way back, by way of passing time and trading gossip, Titus told me everything he knew about what was weird and wrong about Heaster Junior's will.

Heaster's daddy, a man of the same name, had owned a couple hundred acres there in that county. He'd bought some of it, and some of it had been offered to him as a commission after the American Revolution. Rumor had it, he'd worked with Daniel Boone on the Wilderness Road, cutting through Virginia up to the big brine lakes in Kentucky, around where I grew up.

~•~

I didn't know if that was true or not, though. Everybody and his brother in Kentucky makes some claim on Boone. Everybody knows someone who knew him, or worked for him, or put him up for the night. Everybody claims they're kin to him, somehow down the line. And as I heard it, Daniel was one of a dozen kids or so—and he had ten or twelve of his own. So I'm not saying everyone's lying, I'm just saying that lots of people can say things that might be hard to prove.

But as I know it, Boone got around all over the Commonwealth. He liked to cut his name into trees and rocks when he went surveying for the government, and it was his job to explore the territory and clean it up for living on. So it's possible Heaster Senior worked for him at some point.

I'm not saying it's a fact.

But one way or another, Heaster Senior ended up with a whole passel of property, and all it took was a few generations to fill it up with the squabbling families that produced me and Titus.

And when the old man died, his holdings went to Heaster Junior.

Heaster Junior was 99 years old when he finally passed, or that's how Titus counted it. It's a wonder we tend to be such a long-lived bunch, given how little we ever had to eat and how little medicine we ever got. When I think about my own children now, living in good farm country, with good farm food and even a doctor when they need one…I think that maybe, Lord willing and the creek don't rise, they'll live to see a century themselves without any trouble.

But those men, the Heasters (as folks used to call them collectively, when they were both alive), they were tougher than leather.

Now they're both gone. It's like the end of a chapter in a history book.

Don't misunderstand me. It didn't break my heart that they weren't around anymore. I never knew Heaster Senior; he died before I was born. But Junior? Junior was a mean old devil.

Deep down I know that once, Heaster Junior must've been a young man. Once, he must've been a little boy, and maybe he laughed or giggled at his momma or his sisters. Maybe once he picked a flower or roughhoused with a puppy, and maybe once he'd been a handsome young man.

But as long as I knew him, he was ancient and hateful. If there was any good reason for how mean he was, I never heard it.

Some people said it was because he never had any sons, just those four girls. Some people said he'd got his heart broke by a woman. My mother said his ornery spirit was due to the way he'd turned away from God, and he was getting the happiness he deserved; but my mother would say that about anyone she didn't like.

Maybe there wasn't any good reason.

Anyhow, he beat his first, second, and third wives—and he would've beat the fourth if he hadn't been so old and frail by the time he married her. He hit his girls to the point of crippling the oldest one, and she walked with a cane the rest of her life. He'd ride a horse to death just because he felt like it. He shot two of his sons-in-law, but he only killed the one and the justice of the peace agreed it must've been self defense. Of course, that justice would've agreed the moon was made of cornmeal with Heaster standing over him with that rifle.

In the end, Titus figured it was pneumonia that got him, or maybe consumption. The last few years he'd had a hard time breathing, and sometimes he'd take to bed for a month. Every time this happened, everyone would get all excited, thinking this was the end.

And when it finally came, everyone was surprised. I guess by then they'd known almost 200 years of living under the reign of a Heaster, and when Junior was gone, no one quite knew what to do about it.

No one had liked him, but he was the closest thing the valley had to an authority figure. And now he was dead, and it dawned on everybody that he owned all the land we ever lived on, fought on, or fought for.

With him gone, who would be in charge?

Years back, probably before he'd married the missus number four, he'd drawn up a will. Everyone knew he'd gone to Lexington and talked with a lawyer. Everyone knew he'd drawn up some papers and that someday, when the devil came to claim his own, the valley would belong to somebody else.

And this is what I meant when I said something was wrong and weird about the will: no one could find it. It's not that no one knew where it was; according to Titus, within the hour everyone knew where it was. But no one was willing to go and get it, and according to the instructions left by the Lexington lawyer, no one was allowed to go and get it until everyone got there. I'm guessing that this was fine by pretty much everyone, because no one wanted to go into the Witch's Pit, anyway.

That's right. The crazy old bastard hid his will somewhere in the cave on the back acres of his property.

Why?

I'll be damned if I know. I can scarce imagine how he would've got it there in the first place, unless he paid someone a whole ton of money to deposit it for him. If that's how he did it, he must've gotten someone from outside the valley to do his dirty work. Otherwise we'd have heard about it by now. Nobody in the county, not Mander or Coy or anyone else, can keep a secret.

But that's the big news from Leitchfield. Heaster Junior's dead, and his soul is in the Lord's hands or Satan's, but his earthly holdings are up for grabs.

Titus and I both got jumpier as the roads got more familiar on the south side of the Ohio River.

He said his brother told him they'd had a dry year, and I could see it as we rode. The hills were gold and green instead of that richer color I remember from being young; and the forests were looking sparse, with their canopies thinned and brittle. It added to the overall sense that this was a dying, desolate place. It reminded me even harder how much better my new life was, and how right I was to flee in the first place.

Titus didn't say anything much about it. I wasn't sure he felt as happy about his new circumstances as I did about mine. Chicago sounded like a crowded, dirty place, and I don't believe I would've cared for it.

But he piped up when we crossed into the county, and he pointed over his horse's ears. "You know what we're on right now, don't you?"

"Wilderness Road," I said. "North part of it, anyhow. Isn't that right?"

"That's right," he nodded. "And you know what that means."

I answered, "We're almost…there." I'd started to say, "almost home," but that would've made me mad, so I didn't.

We led our horses off the main stretch of Boone's Road and cut off between two limestone hills covered with broken slabs and half-fallen trees. We were dragging ourselves, urging the horses to be careful even though the horses were just fine with the terrain. We were slowing them whenever we could.

But eventually, we did arrive at Heaster's home.

We tied up the horses outside, and wished we could stay with them. They acted nervous. I never in all my life wanted so badly to turn around and run as I did that day.

Heaster's home was the biggest in the valley. He had the most money and he lived like it, even though he wasn't really a wealthy man. When I was a boy, he looked like the richest man in the world, which goes to show how everything's relative.

The house was built into the side of a hill to help keep it cooler in the miserable, fire-hot summers; and I bet it kept the place warmer

during the bitter blue winters, too. It had a big, full porch that stretched all the way across the front, and the whole thing was unfinished wood that was a hundred years old, so it wasn't any particular color anymore. There were three windows, but only two of them had any glass.

The front door was open, and an older woman was standing there, holding it aside with her hip. She stood every bit as firm, dour, and determined as any general. She had to. She was the only thing standing between *them*.

One side of the porch was packed with Coys, and the other side was crammed with Manders.

Divvied up like that, the differences between the clans were more obvious than they might've been otherwise.

Both ends of the family made tall, thin men and petite women, but the Coys were a little more ginger. Their beards were lighter and touched with orange like mine, and most of them had brown eyes. There's a hawkish look to them, especially when they get older. It's something about their noses, sharp and long, and the way their chins aren't very strong.

The Manders are darker, with rounder faces and hair that shines blue-black instead of chestnut. Their eyes are blue too, almost down to the last of them. Their skin goes brown in the sun instead of pink, like the Coys.

They stretched themselves as far apart from one another as the porch would let them, and as far apart as that woman could keep them.

It took me a minute to recognize her as one of Heaster's girls. I say "girls," but that's just a habit. She's old enough to be my grandmother, if she's a day. I wasn't sure which one she was until she came away from the door to acknowledge me and Titus, and I saw she was holding that knobby old cane she always used.

"Ma'am," I said.

"Ma'am," Titus echoed.

We both tipped our hats at her, and she nodded her head at us. I've never been any good at numbers, but I think she must've been in her mid-seventies, at least. She was Heaster's oldest, Abigail.

"Fellas," she greeted us. She squinted, but whether it was from the sun or suspicion at seeing the pair of us side by side, I couldn't say. "Both of you've had long trips, and here you are arriving together. It's a good sign, I believe."

Heads bobbed slowly, uncertainly on each side of the family line.

Titus and I climbed the stairs because it seemed like that's what everyone wanted. Then we looked at each other like we didn't know what to do next. There was a pull like gravity coming from each pack.

I wanted to stand up and say, "You know what? This is all a bunch of horseshit. Me and Titus have been traveling together now for days and days, and I think he's an all right fellow. And anyway, all of us are kin and no one even remembers why everyone fights anymore."

And in his eyes I saw something similar, like maybe he wanted to say something too. But he didn't, and neither did I. The old habits, Jesus help me. They're heavier than chains.

We parted ways, stepping apart and going off to stand by our closer relations. I felt stupid about it, and I could tell by the look on Titus that he did, too. But what were we supposed to do? You don't just leave for ten or fifteen years and then come back, and act like *you're* different—so everything else is different too.

It isn't. Everybody knows it, and you only look like an idiot if you fight it.

Titus and I hadn't bonded so close in a couple of weeks that we thought we were best friends and we could stand up for each other. We were smarter than that.

Once we'd been sorted by the pressure of our families, the rest of them relaxed a little. This was normal. This was better, us on our side, them on theirs. I thought, "What a stupid state, when a whole clan of people is happiest knowing who hates who—and it's easier than thinking maybe some of them are getting along." But I didn't say it.

Instead, I just watched Abigail act like a fierce shepherd with a flock of crazy sheep. She used her body to keep us apart, and I believe everyone was grateful for it. Except for her, nobody talked.

"This ain't everyone," she observed. "I already heard-tell that they couldn't find Gregory, and my sister said she didn't give a shit what came of this whole thing, so she won't be coming either. John was sent for, though, and I think he might come."

"John?" I asked, because there are a bunch of Johns and I didn't know which one she meant.

"Your uncle. I believe he's on his way."

I didn't ask how she knew that, and I didn't ask where he was coming from. Everyone knew about my uncle, John Coy. His brother Abraham went up to find him, back before I'd left. When Abraham returned, he said John had gone crazy up north, and he'd started talking to dead people and obviously, the man had sold his soul to Satan. Let him stay gone, that was what the rest of the family said.

And now they'd called him back?

I didn't ask. Even if Abigail knew why, she might not tell me. Family politics were tricky, and I'd been out of the valley for too many years to just jump back in.

I felt intensely alone, standing there allied with kin I hadn't seen in over a decade.

My mother, gone. I was relieved about that, but I was still real aware that she wasn't present. My sister, gone years and years before. I wondered what she'd look like if she'd lived, or stayed. I spied a cousin roughly the age she would've been, and I tried to imagine her with Winnter's face, but I couldn't do it.

I recognized a few people, or I thought I did. But I didn't see anybody I'd ever been close to.

Across the way, I saw Titus doing the same thing as me—scanning faces, hoping for some reception apart from blank stares and curiosity. He didn't find it any better than I did. I don't know where his parents were, and if any of his brothers were there, I couldn't pick them out.

All told, there were maybe fifty people crowded onto that porch. I don't know how we all fit there—much less how we all fit, and managed not to touch each other at all.

Abigail said to me, "Meshack, when John finally comes, you can catch him up, all right?"

"All right," I said, even though it made me nervous. I never knew John very well when I was a boy, and hearing about the devil-worshipping thing didn't make me too inclined to buddy up with him, but if someone had to, then it could be me.

I saw how she was doing it, penning the outsiders together.

She planted the end of her cane down hard and planted one of her feet down straight, bracing herself to address the lot of us. And she said, "Everybody here has heard part of what's happened, and some of you know more than others. The long and short of it is this—my daddy's died, and there's a proper will, but I can't show it to you because I don't have it. Granny don't have it either."

She meant her stepmother, Opal. Opal was eighty years old, give or take, and she kept mostly to the bed.

"Before he passed, he told us to get the Bible down from the mantle and to see about the twenty-third Psalm. And when we opened it up to that chapter, we found an envelope with some papers in it. The papers said that the will was made in Lexington, but it weren't there no more. If Daddy wasn't pulling our leg, then it's stashed somewhere inside the Witch's Pit."

Folks on both side made murmurs like they'd heard it same as I had, in a rumor, and they'd expected it, but it still surprised them to know it.

"Here's how Daddy wanted it to happen: he picked out six folks—three from each family—and he wanted them to join up together and go down into the hole and get the will. He said that if y'all couldn't stop fighting while he was alive, he'd force you to work together with his dying. And I know you're all wondering if that means he split the land up good, and I have to tell you, I don't know. All I know is that there's a will, and that you'll have to go and get it. He named the six he wanted, and I think that's likely because you're the six set to receive land, but there's no telling until we see the papers ourselves."

She shifted on her feet, adjusting the cane again and bringing it down again, like she was tapping a time with what she was saying.

"For now, though, there ain't going to be no fighting. There ain't going to be no feuding, there ain't going to be no stealing or killing. There just *ain't*. I'm tired of it, and Daddy was tired of it too. I don't care who did what or why, it don't matter. All of you, now, have got to get along—at least until we see where the land goes. If it don't look fair and you want to fight some more afterwards, then I don't give a shit. But for now," she beat the cane against the porch. "For now, like it or not, *all of you is kin*."

She turned on her good foot and went back inside.

Before she shut the door, she poked her head around it and added, "If John ain't here by tomorrow night, we'll pick somebody else to go in his place. Otherwise, we're going to sort this out and settle it up on Wednesday morning. Everybody go, and come back here then."

The old slat-panel thing creaked and cracked when she jammed it closed behind her.

VI.

Back Into Darkness

I KEPT THE LETTER IN my jacket pocket, and sometimes I would pull it out again, just to feel the paper and stare down at my name on the envelope. A thousand times on the train down south I ran my fingers over it and thought, "What am I doing? Why am I following these preposterous instructions, calling me back?"

Twice, when the train pulled into a station in some wilderness backwater, I gathered my things and prepared to leave.

"I can't do this," I said to the man sharing my compartment.

I took my suitcase and I made it to the edge of the ironwork stairs that would allow me to disembark, and I felt the envelope burning against my chest.

So insistent, so vengeful, so reluctant to be ignored.

I turned around both times and went back to my car, where my fellow passenger was too polite to comment upon my inconstant nature.

As the engine dragged us along the rails, the puffing smoke and clanging wheels and whistling steam created a rhythm that lulled me, and from time to time I would rest my neck against the back of the seat and I would dream.

But the dreams were fierce and unpleasant, and I would jolt awake with apologies to my seatmate. The last time I awakened before my final stop, he was gone. Perhaps I was drowsy or dazed, or perhaps I was too overcome with emotion to remember things correctly—but I swear, I spent half an hour wondering if he'd ever been present at all. I tried to recall his face, his clothing, or his luggage, and none of it had left any impression at all in my mind.

This engendered in me a sense of profound and distressing paranoia. My dreams grew more feverish and my impatience became almost unbearable. I wasn't impatient to arrive, but I was impatient to see some end to my torment. I wanted to return to Leitchfield if only to see the visit accomplished, and completed, so that I might never need to attempt it again.

I do not remember any of those dreams except for the last one, the one that was interrupted by the whistle that noted the Lexington depot.

I was tethered to the letter as if by a magical poison. It was drawing me along a course, scorching a path into the earth and into my life; and if I attempted to deviate from the letter's agenda, I would feel a terrible shock and a revolting wave of dizzying nausea.

I *knew*, beyond a doubt, that if I were to throw the letter aside I would perish, and perish in agony. I likewise knew (with that dream-certainty which defies logic or reason) that if I strayed from the letter's path that my fate would be the same. There was a hideous inevitability to it all, a sense of being trapped, penned, and tormented by some predestined appointment or condition.

The train's whistle was a reprieve. I jerked from my seat and seized my personal effects.

In my pocket, the envelope approved of this destination and gave me no further pain or grief, real or imagined. I was quivering under my clothes as I adjusted my hat and stepped down onto the platform at the station.

I arranged for a horse to take me the rest of the way, even though I wasn't dressed for one. The roads that go back to the valley aren't easy on carts or wagons.

I did not push the horse, which was a pretty brown mare I'd acquired at a reasonable price. Why press it forward? I hadn't the heart to command it any faster over the jutting hills and along the flaking, clattering limestone paths.

The sun was harsh on my shoulders, but it was harsh on everything and I did not feel singled out for abuse.

Everything was the same as last I'd seen it. There were almost no people, and no proper roads. No signs of electricity, or indications of community-serving public works. The valley was much as I'd left it, isolated and dreary, and this year it was also dry. None of the scenery ever achieved the vibrant, rich greens of other parts of the nation, and I've been told it's because of the clay which packs the soil. All the trees, all the grasses and plants—they leech up the brown-blood red and it dulls their natural hues.

I don't know if that's true or not, but it's as good a reason as any for the look of half-death the place perpetually wears.

In my pocket the letter throbbed, or my heart was only pounding from nervousness. A whiff of someone's cooking fire tickled my nostrils. Off around the bend, I heard the steady whacking blows of someone cutting firewood.

My throat began to close up, and my hands squeezed the reins so hard that I was cutting myself with the leather strips. "I can't do this," I told the horse, but she didn't care. "I can't do this, I can't come back."

But by then it was too late. I'd been spotted.

A boy perhaps ten or twelve years old leaped up from behind a tree. I think he must've been hunting, or maybe—if I flatter myself—keeping a lookout for me. He gave a little shout that was part greeting, part announcement, and he tore back over the hill. So there was no giving up, turning tail, or running. Not now.

The horse whinnied and I leaned my heels against her flanks.

Forward was the only way. It was the only direction I could manage, forward, and on to Heaster Junior's place. I didn't know where else to go. I hadn't spoken with my nearer relations in decades; I couldn't impose upon their hospitality, if indeed they had any to offer.

This too gave me a pang of terror. Where would I sleep? How would I eat?

I remembered all too clearly the four naked, cracked, and drafty walls of the shanty in which I'd been raised. Surely it couldn't still be standing, I thought. Though even if it'd been replaced in my absence, any newer structure was unlikely to be an improvement.

I had brothers, yes. And they must have their own homes here. I wondered after Abraham, with whom I'd been…not close, precisely. Well, he'd seemed to hate me the least. And once I had been so blunt with myself about the nature of our affections, I understood that no, I couldn't approach him either.

Heaster Junior had a big place, for a relative value of such things. Or now his widow did, if one survived him.

I would've hated to impose on the hospitality of a widow, but I was running out of ideas and in truth, it must've been weeks since the old man had died. It was a gruesome thought, but I could muster no others.

When I came around the final bend before Heaster's old place, the sun slipped immediately and sharply down a ridge behind me and—fast as that—I was shadowed. It was as if I was riding through a box and someone had shut the lid. Only then, when the blinding hot afternoon rays were snatched away, did I feel the chill seeping through the seams of my clothes.

As always, as forever—the valley is small, dark, and cold. And if I were less kind, I might use it to draw some parallel between its appearance and the minds of its residents.

But they were almost on me. The boy came back around the hill with a man who might have been his father and an older woman with a knobby, hickory cane that somehow failed to make her look weak or frail. I felt like I should know who she was. Her stance was familiar, and her reliance on the cane did not look new to me. I remembered her as a caricature of herself, slim and straight.

One of Heaster's daughters, I concluded, but her name was lost to me. *The one he broke with the butt of his rifle.*

Was it because she'd tried to run?

"John Coy," she said to me, and I was a little ashamed that I couldn't return the specific salutation.

"Yes ma'am," I replied instead and it sounded solid enough. Inside, I feared I was coming apart at the seams. I continued talking because it was easier than sitting on top of the horse and shaking. "I received your message, and I've returned, as you asked."

"You got it from the lawyer in Lexington," she corrected me. "I knew you wouldn't come back if it was one of us what asked you. But you're here now, and in the morning, we can all get started."

"Get started?"

She lifted her cane and used it to point over the next hill. "Started. Daddy left you a task."

"He did?" The prospect of it baffled me. I'd barely known Heaster Junior, except as the almost mythic figure who lived in the big house built into the hill. I knew I was kin to him, same as the rest of us within twenty miles.

She nodded. "It would've been your momma, maybe. Or one of your brothers. But since David died, you're oldest so it falls on you."

I bit my tongue to keep a string of words from spilling past my teeth. My oldest brother had died? When? How? Why didn't anyone tell me? I bit my tongue a second, third, and fourth time.

The old woman was watching me, reading me more easily than I daresay she ever read a book. She didn't smile, and she didn't offer to answer any of my unasked questions. She just waited for me to compose myself, and when I still couldn't find anything neutral to ask her, she pointed her cane in another direction—towards the trees to the west.

"What kin you got left here is pressed for space, and it'll be turning late 'fore long. Take yourself up to your nephew's spot. Used to be your half-brother's place. He's been gone since around the time you left, and his wife's gone too. Now it's the boy's, but he don't live here any more than you do."

My mind raced, trying to calculate which half-brother. I'd had my three full brothers, but my mother died and my father remarried, three times all told, and a younger one on every occasion. When I'd left, my youngest half-sister was still in a cradle.

Again, the woman was watching me, observing my calculations and knowing I needed help with it. This time, she obliged.

"I mean your brother Everett," she said. "The boy's Meshack."

"Meshack," I recognized the name, and an image of a barefoot boy with jutting ribs was raised to match it. But that image was twenty-five years old. The boy would be nearly thirty now.

"He's already settled in. Got here this morning sometime. Came down with his cousin. You know the place I mean, where that house is?"

"Yes ma'am, Granny Gail." Her name burst out of my mouth, spoken before it was properly recalled. Abigail, yes. One of four—all girls, to Heaster's undying aggravation. "I know the place."

"All right then." She put her cane back on the ground beside her foot and walked away. The man and the boy followed her. They might have been her son and grandson, but I didn't recognize either of them well enough to say for certain.

While I rode the next half mile or so out to Meshack's, I tried to reconstruct my mental map of how the family looked. It's not just an important thing; for most of the people who live in the valley, it's the *most* important thing. Knowing where you're placed on the family tree tells you who you are, what you're for, and where you belong. It tells you where you came from, and where you're likely to end up, too. It explains why some people live on this side of the valley and some people live on the other side, and it accounts for who you don't talk to unless you've got a big stick in your hand.

The family map doesn't mention the feud, but you could see it all over.

In my head, I drew the lines as best I remembered them. Heaster, his four girls. Two girls married brothers from the Coy family, two girls married brothers from the Mander family. I think that's where it began, or how it split. And heaven knows, we're all related in some fashion. All of us are cousins, anymore.

I tried not to wonder how we'd made so many generations here. I knew there was some mixing, here and there. Once every blue moon, someone would filter in from outside and become trapped here; but mostly, there was too much blood marrying close for anyone's own good.

I tried not to think about it.

Instead, I spent those minutes between Granny Gail and Meshack trying to dissect my instructions, trying to sort the old woman's words and wring more meaning from them. Meshack didn't live here either. He'd come home too.

So I wasn't the only one who'd left.

But David was dead, and I hadn't expected that. I didn't feel grieved by it, not like a man ought to, I don't believe. It was more that I felt a sense of shock. I suppose I honestly thought that the valley was a place where time stopped for everyone who entered it. No one died, no one was born, no one grew up. I saw it as a blank place, *terra incognita* on a chart with no lines and no arrows. And Everett? Half brother or no, I'd only known him in passing.

The horse led herself to the shack at the end of the way, up the gravel trail.

The sun had another half hour before vanishing, but there in the shadow of the trees and the hills it was dark already. A small light burned in one of the windows. While I watched, the light moved from room to room as if the man who carried it was looking for something.

I wondered if Meshack knew to expect me. I hated to surprise him.

I tied the horse and unloaded her, and I promised I'd return to care for her in a moment. Then I went up to the house and stepped with caution up the rickety stairs. I did not think they should hold me. Under each step, I heard a cracking, splitting noise that warned the worst.

The glow inside stopped exploring, and gathered itself to come to the door when I knocked.

A lanky man opened the door. He'd grown into the tall, slim frame that was common to the Coys, but he no longer looked as if he got that way by starving and stretching. His sleeves were rolled up to his elbows and I saw healthy, harness-tight ropes of muscle there. The sun had painted his face a permanent shade of ruddy bronze which was only accentuated by the fire from the lantern in his hand.

"Meshack?"

"Yes sir," he said. In those two words, I liked what I heard. Oh yes, he had gotten out.

I held out my hand, and he returned the gesture so we shook. "I'm your Uncle John," I told him. "I hope they warned you that I was coming, and I regret the imposition."

"It's no imposition. This isn't my house. Near as I can tell, nobody's lived in it for awhile, and both of us can squat here." He held the lantern up and swung it around. "It's not much. Not much to see, or to sleep on. I must apologize for the condition of the place."

I objected to his apologies, and I told him so. "No, please don't. You said so yourself. Not your house. Not anyone's house. I grew up here too."

Whether he remembered me or not, he knew what I meant by "here." He nodded, as if he wasn't sure how to respond. Finally he said, "You *did* grow up here, didn't you? You were one of them too, once."

"Once," I agreed. "I was one of them. But not anymore," I said, knowing it was a risk. I didn't know how strongly this man still identified with the clan. I didn't know if it would offend him to think I no longer wished to be considered part of the family.

But he did not appear offended. He exhaled, as if the news was a great relief.

"Not anymore," he repeated. "Me either, not anymore. And thank God for it."

VII.

Chosen, and Missed: Reflections from the Road, Daniel Boone, 1775

WE WERE ONLY ANOTHER two miles from the water, and when we reached the river, we were done. We could have finished it in just another few days, though it would've gone quicker if we'd had our full strength and we'd been sleeping better. But knowing the job's end was close made us all work harder. Knowing it was near, and there was an end in sight...it made us all eager, even as exhausted and harried as we were.

Sometimes I swear, I don't know why we bothered to set up camp anymore. It's not as if anyone could sleep, but our bodies would've given out on us if we didn't rest. It was hard, though, with her always watching and hanging close. It was hard, with us getting hungrier every day and there being less and less game to shoot.

Even with our numbers reduced, it took a lot of grub to feed twenty men. And our stores, what stores we had, were mostly ruined by that *thing*. She'd shit on whatever she couldn't steal, like if she couldn't have it, nobody would. It was malicious, is what it was. And it scared me, I don't mind admitting it. It scared me because until I cut that road and met that thing, I'd never seen outright hate from anything on earth except for man.

But she could be outsmarted, I knew that for sure—because she almost got the better of me, but she *didn't.*

We set up our camp in the middle of the road we'd cut, because it was the only spot where there weren't any trees creeping right up on us. We didn't leave her anywhere to hide from us, and she didn't have any good way to sneak up on us, either.

It took over an hour to get our fire burning huge and hot, but when it was lit and blazing, I bet you could've seen it from the moon. To hear tell of it, you might think we were inviting trouble; but the fire was our only defense. It gave us light enough to see her by, and it gave us a circle we could cling to, where she wouldn't or couldn't reach us.

My shirts were pocked with holes singed by flying embers, and my skin was stung in little blisters where the coals burned through. I started wearing my buckskin coat all the time, even when it was so warm, so close to the fire—that I thought I'd faint dead away if I stood there another moment. But it was better than getting licked by the fire, and it was better than getting nicked by that thing up in the trees.

So we made our fire and we sat in the middle of the spot we'd cleared and we did our best to rest.

The sun was going down and we were toppling with it. We sank around the fire, all of us crouching as close to it as we dared, and we turned our backs to it so we were sitting in a circle—facing out. Always, we were facing out, and facing up.

What else could we do?

We'd gotten a little more confident, since she'd skipped us the night before. We thought maybe there was a chance she'd leave us alone. Maybe she wasn't hungry anymore, or maybe she had gone her own way, looking for easier prey. That's what we told ourselves, and those are the possibilities we talked about around the fire; but we weren't dumb enough to believe our own talk.

It's just what you do, when you've got a big bunch of people who are all scared shitless, but who don't want to look bad in front of each other. You talk up how you hope it's going to go. But you brace yourself for how you *think* it's going to go.

We *thought* she'd be back, and we were right.

She was too mean to go away easy, or that's how we felt about it; so when the night got all unnaturally quiet again—and when the fire kicked shadows in funny shapes all the way to the treetops on the outside of our circle...we knew she was coming. The whole forest knew it.

The trees cringed back and sank against their roots. The bugs, and bats, and mice alike all quit scurrying and hid in their holes. I imagined them burying themselves in deep, and closing their eyes against the night.

Foxes have holes, and birds of the air have nests—but the son of man hath nowhere to lay his head.

The old verse came to mind, and it made me think of us. Not that I'd ever compare myself or my men to Christ, but the sentiment rang true all the same. And wasn't that the whole point of sending a Christ in the first place? He came here to be one of us, and to live like one of us. That's the task and duty of a caring God, to better understand His creation.

So He knew what it was like, somehow or another. He'd been where we were, lying out on the ground with no shelter and no safety.

I want to say it comforted me, remembering the words from my old grandfather's Bible, and maybe it did for a bit. But as soon as she came down, bigger than a bear and winged, and taloned with claws bigger than any hawk, I don't mean my faith flew away…but it sure did jump up with fright.

She swooped over us, low enough that we could see her breasts all swinging and swaying, but too fast for us to get off any good shots. With her wings all spread out she glided fast, blocking out the moon for several long seconds. She cast a shadow that shocked us with its size. The air burst up underneath her, her wings pumping like bellows and fanning the fire up hard.

First she gave us a pass. It was one long swoop that woke us up and had us all on our feet faster than she could turn around and come back for a second dive.

By then I had my musket out and it was already packed and ready to fire. My other five men with guns were all ready too, just the same—and when she made a second swoop down across the campsite, they did good. They all held steady, just like I told them, until she was close enough we could count her toes.

It almost distracted me, looking at those feet. The claws were long and curved, and pointed so sharp that the firelight glinted on their edges.

But I fired with the musket and then I pulled my pistol out of my belt and aimed that up too.

I didn't have time to shoot it. She was gone as fast as she'd come, and I didn't want to waste powder on shooting at her shadow, so I didn't.

After she'd passed us that second time, and she was coming to the tip of her arc up there in the sky—before she descended again—we all were holding either an axe or a gun and every one of us was prepared to use it. We had no idea how much heat or lead she could take, but we intended to find out.

We fired in waves and it shocked her, but I don't know how much it hurt her. She jerked in the air; we could see her bulky shadow topple and shake, then dip low to the ground. Then she swung back again, lifting herself up high. But she didn't do it smooth. She didn't glide or even do that funny lilting hop, like when she bounced from tree to tree.

"She's hit," I said, but it wasn't a bragging thing—and I didn't say it with anything like triumph. We'd got her, but that didn't mean she was dead; and it didn't mean she'd stay gone just because we hoped we'd hurt her.

Outside camp, back into the trees at the far side of the road, we heard a terrific crash.

All my men started to mumble, all of us wondering the same thing.

There came more crashing, more thrashing. She was kicking around and injured, at least, if she wasn't dying.

We waited, holding our breath and praying. And finally, the thrashing stopped.

And everyone looked at me.

Well, that was okay. This was my job, wasn't it? Someone had to go check and see. Or maybe nobody had to do it, and we should've left it alone. I guess, looking back, I should've just told them all to settle in for the night and stay close to the fire, because maybe she was dead, and maybe it was a trick.

But there was no way to know unless someone went and looked, and since this was my Road, that someone was me.

I took a minute and I reloaded everything I was carrying. While I worked the horn and the powder, and while I dug out the shot, I told all the men at the fire, "I'm going to go see about it. If she's dead, then good. If she ain't, then maybe I can fix that. I've killed bears bigger than her, and I'll kill her too, if I get the chance."

Little Heaster put up his hand.

"You going by yourself?"

"I'm going by myself," I said. "That's right. There's no sense in everybody looking. You'll all take my word for it, won't you? If I tell you she's dead?"

They all nodded, but that wasn't what the boy meant. He said, "What if you get hurt, or get dead? What if you need some help? You shouldn't do it alone. Let me come with you. I'll hang back, if you want me to. And I won't say nothing unless you need me to. I can look after myself. You won't have to worry about me."

"I know you can look after yourself. I'm not worried about that." I tucked the powder horn back into my belt, all slow-like. I was taking my time because I wanted to put him off, but I didn't know how to do it without making him look bad or feel bad in front of everybody.

And I couldn't think of anything. He had a good point, I knew. I didn't like putting anyone else in trouble's way, that's all. He was the biggest lad we had with us, and he was fast, too. If I wanted to take a helper, he was the obvious pick.

I told him, "You're right. If something happens and I can't get back, someone will need to come tell everybody. But it's like you said, you'll have to hang behind. It won't do any good for anybody if we both get eaten. You only come along to watch, that's all. You get it?"

"I get it," he said. He nodded and didn't smile. I figured he got it well enough.

"Let's go, then."

I reached into the edge of the fire and pulled out a branch big enough to work as a torch. The end of it was all lit up. I motioned for Heaster to do the same, and he did. He shook the loose embers off his stick and held it up.

Together me and the boy went walking away from the camp.

I looked back over my shoulder and saw the men who'd stayed; they were standing in a ring, all their eyes glittering bright in the shaky light of the fire. They were curious and scared. They were restless, shifting back and forth on their feet and trying to see through the dark and between the trees where the thing had crashed down.

It didn't take long for us to lose the light of the camp. We were just a few trees deep into the woods and the light was cut in half, and then cut in half again as more trunks came between us and everybody else.

The woods closed in fast, tall above us and wide around us. They felt thicker than they do during the day, when we can see more than a few feet around us—or however far the improvised torches would cast an unsteady glow.

I held out my arm and made Heaster hang back. He didn't like it, but he understood well enough to do as I asked him.

I wasn't real sure where the creature had landed, so I swept my eyes back and forth and squinted, trying to see farther. The whole world was dead quiet, and I didn't like it—because if she were dead, the forest would come back to life. Or that's what I told myself, anyhow. If she were dead, the woods would've breathed a sigh of relief same as us.

But nothing sighed. Nothing quivered or twitched, and nothing moved—not even the wind.

Heaster dropped one of his big hands on my shoulder. I looked back at him and he was holding two fingers up to his mouth, making a face that said, "Hush." Then he pointed at a spot just outside of where my torchlight reached.

I whispered, "You see something?" He was a whole stack taller than me, and for all I knew he could see farther because of it.

He bobbed his head and pulled his pistol out of his belt with his free hand. I almost did, and then I changed my mind.

She'd already been hit with shot, more than a couple of times. Between me and Heaster, we'd have three more rounds of lead to sink into her; but I didn't believe that'd be enough. And then what? Should we hit her with the torches?

No, I didn't like that any. So I pulled out my axe instead. I switched the torch to my left hand and hoisted the axe with my right. It might not pack the same punch, but I could punch with it over and over again if I had to; and an axe don't run out of sharpness so fast, like a gun goes empty of lead.

Little Heaster had been right. I could see her before I could hear her. She was rolling slowly in a clearing she'd made for herself with her own weight. She lolled around and it looked limp, almost. She looked like she was hurting.

It was real odd the way I could watch her and not hear her. Again I was thinking of owls, and the way they fly without making a sound.

I waved Heaster back, and this time he resisted me a little. He only took a half step away, and he didn't stop coming after me. I stopped, and I held out a finger and pointed at him hard.

"Stay here," I breathed. "And if you move without me telling you, I'll shoot you myself rather than let her have you."

I twisted my fingers around the axe's handle. My hands were starting to sweat, so I adjusted my grip on the torch, too.

And then I went to meet her.

VIII.

Six Strangers

UNCLE JOHN SURPRISED ME, not because I didn't know he was coming, but because I was expecting something else. From the stories I heard, I thought he'd look a little more wicked or a little more wild; but the man who came to my dead mother's porch looked more like a school teacher than anything else.

His hair was starting to creep back away from his forehead, and he was lean, like the rest of us. He wore clothes that fit him just right. They looked expensive, and they looked too nice to wear out here. He couldn't possibly work in them.

Or, if he did, it wasn't any work with his hands.

We sat up and talked a little bit. I had some salted meat and dried corn left from the trip down, and I shared it with him while I listened.

He asked about me and what I'd done since leaving, but thatwas a real short story. So mostly, he was the one doing all the talking. I didn't mind. I liked listening to him. I liked hearing someone from Leitchfield speak like an educated man, and the longer he talked the more sure I was that he wasn't some lunatic like I'd heard. The more he talked the more ordinary he sounded, even when he got on about his church.

I'll admit, the bits about the church made me uncomfortable. I haven't been a praying sort of man in many years, but the idea of praying to dead people makes me feel itchy. It doesn't sound right.

But to John's credit, he gathered real quick that it made me feel strange so he changed the subject some. He told me about what it's like living in New York, and how he works up there as a teacher and a counselor, helping folks understand his church. Sometimes he just teaches reading and spelling, but mostly it sounded like he enjoyed telling folks about the church.

I asked if he was something like a preacher in this church. He said it don't work that way. Then he started telling me about circles and chants and spirits, and my face must've told him how I felt about it so he cut himself off.

"That's all right," he said. "I don't mean to make you ill at ease. I just want you to know that it's not something awful or devilish, like I'm sure they told you. Suffice it to say, the world is a big, strange, wonderful place—and there's room for many mysteries. I don't pretend to have all the answers, but I do appreciate having the freedom of spirit to chase down my questions."

"I understand," I told him, even though I didn't understand much of it. I understood that he didn't mean me or anybody else any trouble, and he wasn't worshipping Satan, and that pretty much, he was harmless.

I liked that about him. I didn't get any sense of anger from him, like I did from everyone else in the valley. I just got that same sense of confusion and fear that me and Titus both shared, and it warmed me up a touch, seeing another Coy with that same uncertainty.

The situation being what it was, I couldn't very well confide in Titus or share my worries with him. But John Coy was just as much an outsider as I was, and the name we both wore gave us an excuse to come together.

I wondered after Titus. I hoped he'd found a place for himself, and

I hoped his own people weren't too hard on him. But there wasn't anything I could do for him, so I tried not to worry about it.

We passed the night on the creaking, half-rotted boards of the floor because there weren't any beds and there wasn't any furniture. My other aunts and uncles must've cleaned the place out after my mother died. I don't guess there was any blaming them. They had no reason to think I'd ever be back.

Some deeply set sense of hospitality made me embarrassed that I couldn't offer John anything better. It didn't make sense for me to fret about it, and John didn't hold the house's meager state against me, but still.

All I could do was invite him out to Iowa, and offer him a much nicer place for visiting. He was very kind about it, and said that sometime he'd do his best to come out and see me.

I didn't know if he would or not. There was no telling.

When morning came we were both aching. We'd have been better off sleeping outside on the ground, I bet. But outside it was cool and everything was shining wet with dew when we stepped off the porch, so I decided to be thankful for the roof after all.

Our horses were out back under an overhang that wasn't enough to shelter the poor beasts hardly at all. At least it kept them dry, which was better than nothing. We fed them and mounted them, and took our own sweet time riding back out to Heaster Junior's place, even though we knew we were running late.

We were the last to arrive. People looked at us all impatient-like, but I didn't care too much about that. They were curious, that's all.

Whatever game Heaster was playing from beyond the grave…they could wait a little longer to hear the details.

When I had that thought, I remembered what John was saying the night before, about talking to ghosts. And for a second or two, I almost wished maybe we'd tried talking to some ghosts that last night. Wouldn't that have been easier than all this rigmarole?

Well, maybe not.

Heaster was an ornery old fool when he was alive, and I didn't see any good reason why he'd be different as a ghost. Probably, he'd be even worse. Maybe he'd even take to haunting people he didn't like, just out of a mean spirit.

No. Better to leave all that alone.

If it occurred to John to ask the dead for any assistance, he didn't do it while I was listening—and he didn't tell me anything about it.

Granny Gail was waiting on that porch, still standing up straight and holding real still with that cane in her hand. She made me think of Moses, standing in front of the Red Sea, holding his hands out and parting the water. Only Abigail was so tough she didn't have to lift a finger to hold the Coys and Manders apart; and I swear to you this much, if Moses had to contend with these two families, he couldn't have held them back any better.

"Ma'am," I greeted her, and John said the same.

"Fellas," she greeted us back.

She leaned forward on that cane and placed herself in the center of the porch, between the two groups. She balanced herself there so careful, like a tightrope walker I saw at a circus once. Not too far on this side, not too far on that one. Everything falls down if it leans.

She said, "Now we got everybody here."

John and I found ourselves in the center of a widening circle.

Not all the family members would fit on the porch, so they were spilling out and down the stairs, and into the front yard where we'd brought the horses. Titus was saddled up too, and he gave me a nod that said ‘hello’ without committing to anything more than that.

Two men were also mounted on horses beside Titus, and there was another man—somebody I didn’t recognize right away—who stood beside a horse, and a bit apart from the Manders.

“This is how it’s gonna go,” Granny Gail announced, and there wasn’t a soul alive who’d have argued with her. “John Coy, you’re the oldest man going, but that don’t put you in charge of nothing. You’re going to the Pit on behalf of your daddy and your brother, ‘cause neither one of them’s living no more. Meshack Coy, you’re riding for your mother who ain’t here no more. Carlson Coy, you ride for yourself, and for nobody else.”

Carlson Coy, yes. He was a cousin, and not one too close, I didn’t think. He pulled himself up into the saddle and nudged his foot against the flank of his spotted white pony. He was older than me, not by much; but sometimes it was hard to tell. I’ve heard that hard work will age a man, and maybe that’s true. Living in the valley, though—that’ll age a man like nothing else. His clothes were clean but old, and he was wearing shoes that hung a little loose on his feet.

He adjusted his hat, tipping it our way and moving the pony over to join me and John.

“Titus Mander,” she continued, “You ride for your parents, since neither one of them’s with us no more. Jacob Mander, you ride as Heaster asked; and your son Nicodemus rides for your father, who ain’t well enough to go.

“All six of you, now—you’re doing this for your families and for yourselves, and if you want to do it right you’ve got to set your old gripes down. Put them aside, or God damn the lot of you.”

The way she said it, it sounded like she was finished. But Jacob Mander stopped her from walking away by asking, “Granny Gail, where do we go once we get inside? Ain’t nobody been in there for years, or not nobody who’d admit it.”

“And I ain’t either,” she snapped back at him. “I’ve done told you all there is I know. I don’t know where he put it, and I don’t know why he wanted you all to go down there together. I think the whole thing's as stupid as a shit-pie, but if it don't happen, then that'll just mean more fighting, and that's even stupider. I'm sick of it. And if any one of you had a lick of sense, you'd admit you're sick of it too."

"Ma'am," Uncle John tried to interrupt her.

She ignored him, and didn't let him talk any. "Maybe you folks deserve each other, and that's all it is. If you can't get your act together and behave like grown men, then you deserve to bicker like babies until the day you die. Now go on out, the six of you. Go find my daddy's will, and whatever it says, you're all going to abide by it 'cause you ain't got no choice."

She stomped back inside and slammed the door.

Nobody went after her. Those of us on our horses just sat there, because not one of us wanted to go out to the Witch's Pit even a little bit, but we didn't have a choice in the matter, not anymore.

The crowd of relations around us thinned, or the folks milling around down by our horses backed off even farther. It was a lot of pressure, all of a sudden, and it was making us all tense. The horses even got wind of it, and they started fussing in their reins.

I couldn't stand it, all the standing around. So I led my horse over to Titus's mount, closing the gap between the two sides. And I said, "Cousin, it's been a whole lot of years since I went out to that Pit. I ain't been there since Winnter went missing, and everybody here knows how long ago that was. Does any one of you want to take the lead?"

"What are you doing?" Carlson asked, cross with me already, but I didn't care. We might've been closer kin, and that was a fact; but I wouldn't have known the man on sight and I knew enough of Titus to like him all right.

Titus wasn't dumb, though. He said, "Hey there, Carlson. It's fine, if you want to lead us on out."

"Who says it's fine?" And now Jacob was in on it—this crazy little stand-off of who gets to be in charge.

"*I* said it's fine," Titus said. Everyone got all quiet, because of how he said it loud and with an order lying inside it somewhere. He was only about as old as Nicodemus. Jacob had seniority over him, but Jacob didn't answer back.

I looked over my shoulder at Carlson, who was glaring at the whole bunch of us with a look on his face like he was sucking a lemon. I told him, "Carlson, someone's got to get started. And it don't have to be us. If we can't ride our horses in a line together, we sure as hell can't get ourselves into the cave. So stop it now, I'm asking you."

"You been gone too long, both of you," he said, but he didn't mean me and John. He meant me and Titus.

"Then maybe this'll work after all," Titus answered before I could. "Meshack, me and you can work together all right, can't we?"

"I believe we can. And my uncle here, John. He's willing to get along with the rest of you too, ain't he?"

John nodded and said, "I am."

I pointed my finger back at Carlson, and then swung it around at Jacob and Nicodemus, just so everyone would be real clear on who I was talking to. "That's three of us who ain't about to kill each other. The other three of you get on board, and we'll get started."

The remaining three grumbled, but everyone was watching—even Granny Gail. Or she was listening anyway, we could be sure of that. I don't think any of us would've been ashamed to admit we were a touch afraid of her. And if that was all it took for us to behave there, in front of the house, then that was all right by me.

But the other three men were still shuffling in their saddles, searching the faces of their nearest relations and looking for answers, or permission for something.

It was John who spoke up next. "Don't you see what's happening here? This is a golden opportunity. This is a gift, from Heaster—even if he meant for it to be an inconvenience, it's a *gift*. If it works out, there doesn't have to be any more fighting, and no one has to lose any face. You can all step back away from it, and be even. Isn't that better than the old give-and-take you've been carrying out for the last forty years?"

His questions did not do what he wanted, I don't think. It was because he used big words, and because he'd lost a lot of the accent that marked him as being local to the valley.

"Shut your mouth, John," Carlson said, every bit as nasty as one of the Manders might've said it. "This ain't no goddamned opportunity for shit. It's a stupid game Heaster's laid down, and if you don't know it, then that just goes to show."

"Goes to show what?" he asked, then his lips pressed together tight.

"How you ain't got no business here. I don't care who your momma and daddy were. You shouldn't have come. They should've picked somebody else."

"Cut it out," I told Carlson.

"He's a devil worshipper," Carlson said back, as if that answered anything.

So I said, "He ain't, and even if he was, it wouldn't matter none. He's the one who's owed the money, or property, or whatever else it turns out to be at the end of this thing. He's owed, same as you're owed."

John had been gone away longer than I had. He'd been gone longer than any of us, and even though he was oldest, that meant he had the least authority.

I didn't like the thought of that so much, for a couple of reasons. For one thing, John might've been an outsider through-and-through, but he wasn't no dummy. I've always believed that smart men were worth hearing, and I was afraid that I was on my own in that opinion. But for another thing, if we were counting up status by who'd been gone the longest, then I had the second-least amount of authority, and nobody would listen to me, either.

But for some reason, they listened well enough. Might've been the rest of them were impatient to get started, same as me. Might've been something else. I don't think they shut up and started riding just because I recommended it, but that's what happened.

One by one, the Manders set out ahead of us. Titus brought up the rear of their clan, and I went to swing my horse in behind him, but Carlson nosed his horse in faster. I don't know why it mattered for him to go first. I let him do it, and I offered to let John go in front of me. He fussed about it, but I insisted.

I wanted to watch the rear of our little train.

I assumed we might get followed, and I wasn't sure how friendly our followers would turn out to be.

And you know, I liked John and I thought he was a real smart man. But I had some doubts about how well he'd hold up if a brawl happened, and I didn't bet he'd be any good at keeping lookout.

He led the horse on into the line, in front of me. He looked over his shoulder as he did it, though, like he was watching me for some signal. I didn't know what he wanted, so I couldn't give him the answer he was hunting for.

That's how we made our march out to the cave, anyway. We rode all in a line because most spots, that was the only way the horses could pass through the narrow places, or through the tight wedges between broken-off hills.

Jacob Mander rode first up front, with his son Nicodemus behind him.

Then Titus, then John, then me.

IX.

To the Bottom of the World

THE OTHERS SINGLED ME out, but I suppose that's not surprising. I am the oldest, yes. And I've been gone the longest, true. And my beliefs have diverged from theirs quite significantly—there's no denying it.

I wonder if that's where the real rub lies.

Meshack is younger, and stronger, and a little closer to this place. It startled and upset me to see how swiftly his sturdy, specific way of speaking relapsed into false contractions and low expressions when he was confronted with the families. But then I realized that it is no weakness, and no affectation. He interacts with them better when he speaks their language, and his self-imposed exile has lent him authority over them.

I do not think he realizes it. I think he was shocked when the other riders obeyed him.

Titus looked equally astonished at being obeyed by members of his own clan; and if he doesn't learn to better hide his surprise, he'll lose that power before he's learned to wield it.

We arrived at the Witch's Pit around midday, but it took hours to set up camp. I'd forgotten the extent to which the old biases run so deep, and how even the smallest task is a chore. Every small event, and every small job was a challenge to someone's honor, someone's family, or someone's pride.

It was ridiculous.

"The fire ought to go somewhere over here," Jacob said, lashing his horse to a low branch on a near tree. He pointed at a spot close to the edge of the cave's entrance.

Carlson pointed a few feet in another direction. "Don't be daft. That close to the mouth, and we'll smoke ourselves out before we ever get inside. We need to put it farther off, closer to the center."

He meant the center of the clearing.

Around the entryway to the Witch's Pit there was a wide swath, so neat and bare that it might've been cut that way on purpose. The surrounding grass was low and brown; it wasn't stamped or crushed, it had merely withered in a loose and swirling pattern that spewed outward from the cavern.

I've heard it said that a cave is a living thing, and that it has its own breath, and blood, and systems. But I've also heard that the air inside can go rancid and poisonous, given time and lack of room to circulate.

And that's what I recalled, standing beside my horse and facing the ink-black crevice on the side of the hill.

I imagined a hole in the world that breathed out noxious, killing vapors.

Jacob stepped away from his horse. "It can go right over here. That cave's so big and deep, we're not going to smoke a damn thing out. And we don't want to stick it too close to the trees."

"It figures," Carlson said. "A Mander don't know how to make a fire in the forest without burning the place down."

Titus took two long-legged strides and set himself between them before it could go any further. It astonished me how swiftly he moved, and how instinctively and immediately he understood how fast these things could escalate.

"Both of you old assholes shut yourselves up."

Nicodemus joined in then. "Whose daddy are you calling an asshole?"

"Now don't do that," Titus told him. "Don't do it. I'm calling asshole any man who tries to start a stupid fight for no good reason except he wants to hit something. You two step back and leave each other be. We got a job to do, and we're gonna do it—even if it means three of us have got to tie the three of you to one of these trees and leave you there."

I heard the click of a gun's hammer cocking. Not half a second later, I heard two more. I froze.

I believe that Nicodemus drew first, but I can't say for certain. I do know that Jacob had drawn up too, and that Meshack was right alongside them.

Meshack's gun was newer and brighter, and it was much larger. I have to say it was some sort of rifle, but I've never been terribly interested in firearms and I don't know much about them.

The long gun got everyone's attention. Both of the smaller guns were aimed at it, and while they were pointed away from Carlson, he drew his own stubby revolver and stood to the side. For a moment I was uncertain who he meant to threaten, but his family loyalties won that battle. He went shoulder to shoulder with Meshack.

"Gentlemen, please!" I said. I held up my hands and tried to move closer, but I was shaking with terror.

"Stay out of it, John," Meshack growled from the side of his mouth. I don't think he was angry with me. I think he meant to protect me, for I was the only man present who was unarmed.

"No, I can't. I may be old and unarmed, and you all may think I'm uncommonly strange, but this is my problem too, same as it's yours. What if it ends here, like this? What if you kill one another, all five of you?"

No one answered me, and for all I knew none of them were even listening to me. Their eyes were narrowed and unblinking, twitching back and forth between one another. I could see them making their calculations, making their bets. They were guessing and gauging whose gun or aim was most likely to fail, and whose was most to be feared.

So I continued. "You make Heaster right, if you die this way. You make that despicable old man right. He thought you couldn't do it. And those people you left back at his old place, they don't think you can do it either. Is that how you want this to end? Or would you prefer…"

A shadow flickered fast, past the spot where I could see clearly out of my eye's farthest corner. I blinked and tried to see it better without taking my stare away from the men with the guns.

He was smallish for a man, but he walked like a big fellow. He was walking like a man who was comfortable, in a world where he was master and Adam and king.

As soon as I'd gathered this much, he was gone—and there was no sign that he'd been there at all.

Jacob risked giving me a look, since he was facing me anyway and it didn't cost him any safety to do so. "Something wrong with you, devil-worshipper?"

"No," I said quickly. Just as quickly, I decided against defending myself of the charge. "I'm only distracted, and distressed. All of you know it—that I'm not a man who knows how to hold a gun. I haven't seen one fired since I lived here last, and they make me… uncomfortable."

I was admitting too much weakness and I knew it. I changed the subject. "You can make that old dead bastard right, or you can make a liar out of him. This is your chance to be men, and not squabbling boys, kicking over one another's toys. You're smart men. All of you are. Now *act* like it, for heaven's sake. Meshack," I said to him, imploring him—because he was the one I knew best, and trusted most.

"Meshack, put the gun down. Titus, I know the two of you are friends, or almost friends. Blessed are the peacemakers," I said, searching for the familiar old phrases that were so far lost to my memory. "For they...blessed are the peacemakers."

"For they shall inherit the earth." Nicodemus was the one who finished the verse. He didn't lower his gun.

"In my experience," Carlson said, "the peacemakers inherit the earth a little too early for their health." He didn't drop his gun either.

Meshack said, "He's right."

"Meshack," I tried again to appeal to him, but he shook his head.

He told me, "No. It's different here. It's *still* different. I know you're trying to help, but you just don't remember."

I was prepared to argue with him. I opened my mouth to do so, but then I closed it again. The man was back; he was right there, beside the mouth of the cave. He wasn't watching the stand-off.

He was staring at me.

I stared back. What else could I do? He was the first ghost I'd ever seen, and I couldn't take my eyes away.

I knew he was dead. He *had* to be dead. The living have sharper edges. They take up space. They don't make the air around themselves hum and quiver, like the hot surfaces of an oven curdling the air in a kitchen.

The details were hard to discern. He was not very tall, but he was brawny and wide-shouldered. His suit hung heavy on his limbs; it wasn't cotton or wool. It had more density and less *give*, and I thought it might be buckskin—like the Indians sometimes wore.

He pointed at a spot off to the side of the cave's maw. There was a place where a pair of trees grew up against the sheer face of the hill, their roots winding between the rocks.

And then he wasn't there anymore.

"What are you looking at?" Jacob demanded. He could see me best; as I said, he was facing me—looking over Meshack's shoulder I was directly in his line of sight.

"I'm not...not anything," I breathed. I wrenched my gaze away from the cave and confessed very slightly, "I only thought I saw something."

"What?" Meshack asked without turning around to look at me.

"Someone," I clarified, but not completely. "Gentlemen," I appealed again. "Please. No guns. Let us do this task, prove our terrible patriarch a liar and a fool, and return to our homes."

I looked at the hillside wall again.

Jacob let the barrel of his gun droop. I couldn't win them with reason, but I could distract them with curiosity. I made note of this, as the other barrels tipped until they all pointed at the ground.

The eldest Mander quit looking at me and then did something that Meshack later assured me was quite brave: he turned to see the spot that so deeply occupied my attention.

"There ain't nothing there," he correctly observed.

"I could've sworn I saw something." I took the moment of relative peace to move behind them and around them, over to the place where the dead man had stood. I lifted my right leg and propped myself against it. I leaned against the hill and around its side, as much as I could. I ran my hand along the rough bark of the tree and tried to engross myself in this activity—anything to calm myself. My heart was still racing from the near-chaos of the moments before; but by the sounds of things, the rest of the men had already returned to their prior, more manageable levels of strained discord.

"What're you doing?" Meshack asked. He was the first to join me, and I'd guessed right—he'd already slung his rifle back over his shoulder, into a holster that was strapped there. The sun glinted off the long, fierce-looking thing, and I winced to see it so close. Behind us, I heard the reluctant clacks of the other guns being un-primed, and re-holstered.

"I thought I saw something. And now I think I've *found* something," I announced.

The other four men crowded around as tightly as they could without actually touching one another. They leaned around me. We peered between the trees, at the V in the fork where the trunks grew apart.

Carved into the rock, there was a short message. I traced it with my fingers. I scraped out what dirt and lichen I could, until the words were fully revealed.

"What's it say?" Carlson asked.

I'd forgotten that most of them probably couldn't read. So I said the words, sounding them out because the spelling was creative, to put it kindly.

"I can't make out this first part," I admitted. "The rock's too worn. But the rest of it says, 'killed a thing here.' And it's signed. It's says…" I poked my finger against the 'D' and held my breath. "It's signed 'D. Boone.'"

Someone behind me let forth a low whistle, and the men began to murmur.

"Let me see it," Carlson insisted. He put a hand on my shoulder and urged me back, out of the way. Even though most of them couldn't read it, they were going to touch it.

"Would you look at that!" Jacob jabbed his gnarled index finger at the letters. "Would you look at *that*!"

"I'm looking, I'm looking," Carlson said.

The two men were elbow to elbow. They were within one another's breathing space, and they were smiling. Not a minute before, they'd been prepared to shoot.

Their enthusiasm was a true marvel. Meshack craned his neck around too; and he said, "It might be real. You think it's real?" he asked no one in particular, I thought. But then I realized he was aiming one eye over at me.

I started to answer, but Titus beat me to it. "Who else would go to the trouble?" he asked.

Jacob pulled his hat down off his head and punched it happily. "Daniel Boone. You know, I wonder if that don't mean the old stories about Heaster Senior got any truth in them."

cilled a
thing he
D. B

"The ones about him working on the Road?" Carlson shrugged. "It ended not too far from here, up at the river. There's a real good chance Boone passed this way."

Titus was grinning as big as the rest of them. "I bet it's him, all right. I bet he's the one who cut it there. He used to do that, you know. He signed his name on things, when he was exploring. That's how he marked his way."

I didn't know if that was correct or not, but I didn't argue.

"Look how he spelled 'killed,'" Meshack said.

And that was the first I realized that Meshack had learned how to read, somewhere along the line. He couldn't have learned it at home; I wondered where he picked up his education.

Between the bobbing heads crowded around the inscription, I read it again.

...cilled a thing heer
D. Boone

While the men chattered excitedly I wondered also, "Was he the man I saw?"

I knew enough about the man to know the engraving might be real; and I knew enough to understand why my ordinarily cantankerous companions were, for the moment, as excited as school boys. Heaster might've been our literal patriarch, but Boone was the father of us all—the George Washington of our commonwealth.

His creative spelling only made him more appealing. As I understand the lore, he was barely literate, prone to wandering, occasionally violent; and he lived most of his life in fear of debtor's prison due to a score of terrible land speculation deals.

Yet even so, he was a patriot and a warrior. He was the man who cut the Road.

And I don't believe you could find a man in Kentucky who wouldn't say Boone's name with pride.

Had I seen him? Hadn't Shirley told me, before leaving Lily Dale, that the spirits would help me if they could? I struggled to recall the ghost's features, his clothing, or anything else that might give me a clue.

He could've been any explorer. He could've been any woodsman or fellow of the frontier. He could've been anyone.

But he'd pointed at the message as if it meant something.

I looked again at the letters left in the side of the hill, and I clutched at the pocket where I still kept the letter that had summoned me. "Boone?" I whispered. I closed my eyes and inhaled, exhaled, carefully, counting each breath.

When I opened my eyes, there was no sign of him.

X.

Into the Fray: Reflections from the Road, Daniel Boone, 1775

It must've been her feathers that cushioned her against the ground, and against the rustling loud sound of the forest floor crackling and splintering beneath her. But it was so soft, the noises she made—even though she was big, real big. I'd been saying she was the size of a bear, but when I got up close I saw I'd underestimated her by a hundred pounds, anyway. She was the size of a cow, and covered with those long feathers.

I wanted to believe it was a death roll. While I watched her spin, tumbling in a lopsided circle like an egg, it was easy to say she was dying.

With Little Heaster behind me, I came closer. I tiptoed up, trying to sort out the situation. I held the torch over my head, trying to squeeze out every drop of light.

I didn't come too close, not right away.

Underneath her, the ground was wet. Not soaking, but wet. She was bleeding. I couldn't tell what part of her was injured.

She was flexing her wings, over and over, using them to rock herself back and forth, around and around. They weren't bent or shattered so far as I could tell. I'd be pleased if we'd landed a blow to her body. I'd have settled for a broken wing, because at least that'd mean she couldn't sneak up on us from above; but a wound to her torso might keep her from coming back altogether.

She let out a sigh and a groan. The groan croaked wetly, and I prayed with all my heart that she had a throat full of blood.

Her path in the clearing was being worn slower and slower. The spots where she'd flattened small trees and trampled down plants with her bulk were growing darker with red-black stains, and then she let out one more awful groan—or I thought it was a groan, anyhow—and then there was a cloud of gas and a rushing wet flush of nastiness.

And I knew it wasn't a groan. Her bowels had released, and the smell of her runny gray shit and piss mingled with the faint metal stink of blood.

She toppled right through it, smearing the mixture across herself and picking up dirt and pine needles too. Everything she touched stuck to her, even as she was moving, and moving slower. And she rolled...almost to the tipping point of pushing herself for another loop...but then she sagged, and merely rocked back and forth until all the energy was gone out of her.

I couldn't tell if she was dead or not. She'd lolled away from me, her feet sticking up in the air like a bundle of twigs.

The stench of her body stuck in my throat and choked me hard.

I gagged, but I clenched my chest up and tried not to show it. Behind me, Heaster was making soft panting noises, as if he were trying to keep himself from vomiting. I didn't blame him. She smelled even worse up close.

Heaster called out, soft but low enough that I heard him all right. "She dead?"

I told him, "I don't know."

Still holding the torch in my left hand and the axe with my right, I sidestepped around the place where she'd stopped. I stayed as far away from her as I could. But I came around, past the one sprawled wing that had flopped down, the size of a bed sheet. I shuffled past her twisted neck, and around the ruffled crown.

Her face was angled in the other direction, so I had to go a little farther. I pushed my back up against the tree trunk at the edge of her cleared-away spot. I stayed as far from her as I could, while still getting close enough to see.

I stared at her chest. Her flopping gray bosom was sunken, one breast to the right, one to the left until it was tucked where you might say her armpit should be. Even though my arm was getting tired, I swung the torch out—I held it straight as far as I could, until it was almost over her.

It wasn't my imagination. With a small lift and drop of that gore-smeared tangle of feathers, she was breathing.

That was fine. She wasn't dead, and I'd expected that much. But I was uneasy, because she was breathing quickly, one-two, one-two, one-two, like a thing that's been winded by a struggle, and not like a creature about to breathe its last.

I didn't like it. I started backing up, and I said to Heaster, "Draw your gun, boy."

He'd already thought of it. I could see him at the edge of the torchlight, the end of his pistol pointing down at the rounded, filthy, feathered thing that stunk to high heaven.

And then my makeshift torch sputtered. It didn't go out, but it cracked and spit sparks, and it cast off a small spray of embers down onto the creature's face.

One smoldering coal leaped in a white-orange arc to fall against her eyelid.

Her eyelid jerked, and snapped open like a window shutter. Her beak split, and she erupted into a cry so loud and so close that it made my ears ring and hum—and it was all I could do not to drop the torch right there, because I knew I'd been *had*.

If she'd been as weak and as dead as she'd pretended, her breathing would've been slow and hard. If she'd been so close to death, her eyes would've parted some and all her flesh would've relaxed, not just her bowels. I *knew* that. I knew all of it, and none of it had stopped me from going up close, and I felt like an idiot for it.

I leaped back away from her, and I was so surprised when she moved that I forgot I was standing between her and a tree. My right shoulder slammed against a very big trunk, and my feet tripped up in its roots.

But I didn't drop the axe, and I didn't drop the torch. I swung them both out and towards her; I clapped them against each other and more sparks showered into her face—because God help me, her face was on level with mine, just as quick as *that*.

One moment she was on the ground, playing possum, and the next she was on her feet and reaching for me—stretching that frayed-looking neck and biting at me with that beak so sharp it could've cut timber. And all I could think was how I knew she didn't like the fire, so I hit the torch again with the axe-head and more sparks sprayed. Some of them singed my eyebrows and pinked up the skin of my cheeks, but my buckskin coat kept the worst of it off my arms.

I squinted against the sparks because I had to—because I didn't like them, but she couldn't stand them—and that was the only advantage I had against her.

My hair began to cook, adding to the gut-turning stink that filled the night. I didn't pay any attention to it, even when the smoldering strands were charred all the way to my ears.

She was up, and she was angry. That made two of us, and I had the upper hand because I was scared to death on top of being mad as hell.

She lunged, beak-first and snapping.

I held the torch forward and swung the axe underneath it, right around the level of her throat. But she jerked her neck back, limber as a goose, and popped forward again faster than I could raise the axe a second time. I ducked away, knocking my elbow into the tree but not really hurting myself—and once I had the tree behind me, I could sidle around until I had that big old trunk between me and her.

She bit and beaked at the trunk, first left, then right, then back again to the other side.

I hugged the trunk as close as I dared, and I shuffled right, then left, then right again to dodge her. I stumbled over the uppermost roots but I kept my footing pretty well, all things considered.

Heaster hollered something, trying to get her attention.

I said, "Stop it, you damn fool!" Partly I yelled it because I wanted him to stop it, and I wanted him to know he was acting foolish; but partly I did it because I wanted to keep her attention on *me*.

It halfway worked, which is to say she looked back at him but she didn't want to leave me while she thought she had me cornered. He distracted her for a second, that was all.

And that was all it took for me to step out around the side of the tree and land a good, hard crack with the sharp end of the axe. It caught her underneath the eye.

She roared, and it was a different sound than the ugly croaking we usually heard from her. I think it was real pain I heard, and I would've swung again for the same spot except for she swiped me with one of her wings and knocked me out from my spot of temporary safety.

Those wings of hers were impressive. I'd known it before, but I didn't fully understand it until she stood there and held them open—she waved them like cranes do, when they're doing those mating dances, making themselves look all huge to the other birds. Well, she made herself look all huge, all right, and Heaster couldn't pass up the chance to take advantage of it.

He fired, and the report was louder than a cannon there in the half-dark where we fought her.

I don't know what he hit but she arched her back, and her roar took on a screaming squeal. She turned to him, and there was nothing I could do to hold her attention, even though I ran right underneath her, right in front of her, but she had something else to worry about now.

She jumped, and she landed on top of him.

He was a big ol' boy, I've said before. He was a little on the skinny side, but he was tall and heavy enough to swing an axe like a big man, so when she flattened him in that one short hop—crushing down on his chest with those feet the size of bedside tables, it amazed me how swiftly she'd moved in to crush him.

And she was wounded, too! How many times did we have to hit her and shoot her and cut her before she could be stopped?

I didn't know the answer to that question, but I wasn't about to let her have Heaster. I was on her fast as a cat, scared and mad and swinging an axe in one hand and a torch in the other.

She bumped me with her shoulder as I came around to swing and even though that don't sound like much, I mean to tell you it was as hard and heavy as getting struck with a sack of potatoes. The blow threw me off balance but I still landed one good chop and one good thump with the torch.

My torch was getting real beat-up, though, and it wouldn't be long before it was going to go out or get stomped out.

So I started holding it away from her. I needed the light—probably, I needed the light worse than she did—and Heaster was under her, but not pinned as bad as I thought. She didn't have his arms pinned, or maybe she did. But he got one arm free and bless him, it was the arm that was holding his torch.

He brought that torch up to her underbelly and seared a patch there, burning away feathers and flesh and making that bird-thing scream and squeal. She lifted one foot up off his chest.

I'd rolled away from her and was partly on the ground, but when I seen how good Heaster'd got her, I came back swinging again.

She screamed at me, and she moved that other foot off Heaster. He scooted out from under her; I saw his pistol on the ground, but he didn't have any time to reload it and he knew it, so he left it there while I tried to lure her away. The boy had his torch, and he had an axe someplace—I guess he'd dropped it, or she knocked it away.

I found it fast and ducked down to grab it just as her wing came swooping down over him. She missed him, and I thanked God for it.

I was looking at his shirt, and there were punctures all over it, and the holes were running with blood. They looked like bullet holes, but I knew they weren't and I prayed they didn't go so deep. Heaster was standing, anyway. He was standing and he was fairly steady.

"Hey!" I screamed at the thing, because she was looking back and forth between us, trying to back up enough so she could watch us both. "You!" I yelled, and I snagged her attention good.

She took three long strides on those twiggy, sharp-ended feet and I yelped. I held up the axe and got ready to move it, and I held up my torch even though its light was starting to fade. It was all the light I had except for Heaster's torch, and he was far enough away from me that it didn't hardly help.

She reached out, craning that neck that was longer than it looked, and faster than an arrow she launched her beak straight for me.

I thought she was trying to bite me, and I jumped—but she wasn't biting at *me*. She clamped those jaws, those scissor-sharp horns of her face, against my torch and she bit it in half. She snipped it clean out of my hand, as easy as a gardener pruning a rosebush.

I was almost so stunned that I stood there frozen while the lit-up end of the torch dropped down to the ground. My guardian angel was whispering hard into my ear, though, and I leaped backwards before I'd even had a chance to think it through.

M. Geyer

By the time the creature had stomped the torch into the dirt, I was back behind another tree and hiding there like a boy.

"Run!" I shouted to Little Heaster, and I watched his bobbing yellow light weave and wobble between the trees.

The last thing I saw, before the last little glow disappeared, was the creature's head—her neck did a full circle, just like an owl's—and her eyes settled on my hiding spot.

XI.

Into the Cave

Uncle John was acting funny. I mean, he was acting funnier than usual.

It started when he was staring at the mark on the hillside rock wall. How did he know it was there? You couldn't see it, not until you were right up on top of it—and not until you'd pushed away a bunch of dirt and plants.

He stood apart from the rest of us while we got all boyish about seeing what Boone left. After I'd gotten my eyeful, I joined my uncle and said to him real quietly, "That was a strange and lucky thing, don't you think?"

"What do you mean?"

"You spotting that carving over there. Look at them, all getting along."

"It won't last," he said. "You know it won't. They'll forget about it soon enough."

"No, they won't forget," I argued. "They'll go home and tell everyone they see about it. But they'll get tired of getting along, and then they'll snap right back to the old feuding ways."

I was right. Eventually, the friendly happiness we shared from finding the Boone mark was used up; and eventually we made a fire—halfway between the spots everyone was arguing about.

I would've rather set it farther from the cave, but it was either put it where we did or break out the guns for another round. I loved my long rifle, and it was probably the most valuable thing I owned apart from my house in Iowa; but I wasn't in a rush to show it off again.

It was only mid-afternoon and we didn't really need the fire yet. We only made it to mark our spot, and declare our camp. It's just something men do when they stop on the road.

We stood around it, warming ourselves even though we weren't that cold.

"We should go in tonight," Jacob said, hands on his hips, standing like he meant business.

Carlson said, "It's getting late. And we don't know how big the cave is, anyhow. We should just camp tonight, and bother with it in the morning."

But Uncle John pointed out, "What does it matter if the sun goes down? It's darker inside the cave than outside at night, regardless. Don't let the hours determine how you approach the place."

The silence around the fire confessed without words that he'd said something reasonable.

"Maybe," Titus said slowly. "One or two of us ought to poke our heads in and take a look around—just to get an idea. Anybody here know how deep the Pit goes?"

We all shook our heads.

He continued. "Now, how many of us have gone inside, just a little bit? Most of us have peeked inside, I reckon—even if it was on a dare from our brothers. Meshack," he looked real pointedly at me. "What about your sister? When she took off, did you come in here to look for her?"

I started to say "no" like a reflex, but I caught myself. "We weren't real sure this is where she went," I mumbled. "Just 'cause that's what she told Momma, that don't make it true. But I might've poked my head in, just a little bit."

Uncle John frowned at me, not like he was angry but like he was worried. "I thought you'd never been inside."

I shifted on my feet and folded my arms. "I've never spent any real time in there, no. But when my sister was gone, yeah—I might've looked around. I didn't go so far that I couldn't see the entrance, though, and that don't hardly count."

"It counts well enough," Nicodemus said.

"Well enough to what?" I asked.

"To make you the expert."

"I don't want to be the expert," I said, even as I knew they were right. Even as I stood there thinking about it, small details were rising in the back of my mind, bobbing up like apples in a rain barrel.

"Tough luck," Titus said, but he didn't say it too unfriendly. "Let's talk then, about what we know."

"We've done enough talking for one day," Carlson griped. "I'm sick of talking."

And I griped back at him, "Nobody knows much, so don't worry—it won't take long."

I had an idea. I reached up into a tree and half pulled, half picked a slender branch. I squeezed the small green bits off it and kicked at the dirt until I'd cleared a spot about as big as a pillow.

"Here's what I know, and any man who can add anything should speak on up, and interrupt me if you want to. Right inside there's a big room that splits up two ways." I used the end of my stick to make a rough drawing of it. "I think one of those ways doesn't branch very far. It dead ends pretty swift."

"Which one?" Nicodemus asked.

"I don't know. I only remember hearing about it when folks were looking for Winnter. One of the two main ways dies out, so there's only one way back away from the opening."

Uncle John peered down at my sketch and said, "It's a pity we don't have a map."

"It's a pity we don't have a dead man with better sense than to send us all on a wild goose chase," Jacob complained. "And while we're making wishes, it's a pity I don't have a thousand dollars and a pretty wife."

But John didn't give up so easy. He ignored the mocking and said, "Hasn't anyone ever charted it? Anyone at all?"

"Boone, maybe," I said. "Nobody we know ever went inside too deep. Don't you remember? Folks have been telling stories about this old hole since Heaster Senior first took the land."

Nicodemus said, "The way I heard it, Heaster Senior swore there weren't no cave out here on this land. And when one of his neighbors made a fuss about it, he admitted he knew it was here. But he said it was poisoned air inside, and that nobody should go there. He said we shouldn't play out here, or put any animals inside or anything."

We all looked at the ugly yellow swath of dead plant life that ringed the Pit's entrance.

John swallowed hard. "I remember Heaster Senior, just barely. He died when I was a boy. But he was old then, real old." And for a second there, I heard the valley in his voice. For a second, he sounded like one of us. Then it was gone, as fast as I'd heard it. "I remember hearing him talk about the poisoned cave, and how the air inside it would kill a man or a beast."

His eyes flickered, and darted off to some spot behind me. His gaze settled again down on the fire.

Jacob scowled. "How are we supposed to go in if the air's tainted up like that? I bet it's some kind of trick. I bet that old bastard wanted to kill us all—to take us all with him."

"I wouldn't put it past him," his son said.

"Nobody would," I agreed. "But if someone went inside with the will, then someone survived long enough to leave it. And the air in there stinks, don't it? We can all smell it from here. It's nasty, but I don't think it's deadly."

The other men lifted their noses, and one by one they nodded. The smoke couldn't cover it, not completely. Wafting out from the mouth of the Pit came a sour smell—the smell of something rotting in an outhouse.

Uncle John threw in his two cents. He said, "I think Meshack is correct. The air would sicken us, even out here. It's as foul as can be, but I don't think it'll kill us. Perhaps we should cover our faces with our handkerchiefs."

I closed my eyes so I didn't have to see the other men staring at my uncle like he'd just jumped down out of a tree and started taking off his clothes.

Jacob finally spoke, and he didn't even try to hide a laugh. "John Coy, maybe a *fancy* man like yourself keeps a handkerchief in every pocket. But I'm proud to say I don't own a damn one of the things. We can handle the stink in the hole, can't we, fellas?"

His son and my cousin Carlson laughed, and Titus even smiled.

"Don't worry about it," I said to Uncle John. "We'll all handle it fine. If you want to use a handkerchief or whatever, then that's up to you. Honest, though, I don't know if it'll make a difference. If it smells this bad out here, God knows how bad it'll be inside."

He shrugged, and the teasing rolled off his back like water off a goose. He didn't like it when they made fun of him, but he was determined not to let it upset him—and he did a good job of it.

Maybe he did too good a job of it. Maybe it's easy not to get your feelings hurt when you think you're better than the people who are making fun of you. But if he felt that way, I'm sure it wasn't personal. It wasn't half as personal as the mean things the rest of the family said to *him*, anyway.

Titus looked at me, and his face was real serious. He said, "Does anyone know for sure if there's anything in there at all?"

Nobody did, so nobody said anything. I fiddled with my stick and shrugged.

Uncle John was staring off into the distance again. He broke his own silence and said, "We could send someone in ahead of everyone else, with a torch. Just to make sure it's all right."

"A torch?" Nicodemus said. "What we need is a canary."

"Well we ain't got no canary," Carlson spit on the ground. "And this ain't no coal mine. But I know what he's talking about, with a torch. If the air's too nasty the torch'll go out, won't it? Then somebody goes in first, and if he stays alive and the torch stays lit, then we all go in after."

Jacob waved his hands like he thought all this was completely stupid. "What damn fool among us is gonna go in first?"

Fast, right on the heels of that, Uncle John said calmly, "A man who'd like the advantage of getting the first look." Then he added, just as quiet, "I'll do it, if none of you want to. I've got a handkerchief, after all."

Carlson seemed all right with the idea, but Jacob and Nicodemus went pissy about it. I didn't say anything because I figured my uncle was bluffing. Me and Titus exchanged a look that said he was thinking the same thing, but he wasn't going to point it out.

When the dust settled, it was Jacob who finally agreed out to get first go of it. He was oldest next to Uncle John, he had better eyesight than Carlson, and he wasn't about to let his own boy go first.

And since we didn't know how long this fragile agreement would hold up, we quit fighting over whether or not to go in then, or later.

John had been right anyway. Dark was dark, and it didn't matter if you were inside or out if you couldn't see your hand in front of your face. Besides, it was starting to look like rain. Maybe it'd sprinkle and maybe it'd pour. If we got inside the Pit, we'd be dry.

But first, Jacob was going to check the air and take a peek around.

You couldn't have paid me enough to go first. Not in a thousand years, with my guardian angel standing beside me, if I had one.

I kept thinking about Winnter, no matter how hard I tried not to. I thought about my sister, long dead and maybe left lying inside this cave—or maybe...

...I tried to step on the thought, to crush it out like a cigarette...

Or maybe, what if she was still down there someplace?

That was crazy thinking, and I knew it. But that didn't stop the thinking, no matter how much I figured it ought to. I thought about home, and my wife, and my babies—and the one about to be born. I thought about my fields and my house. I thought about my long, shining gun.

But into the nooks and crannies of these nice things, thoughts of my sister curled like smoke.

In my waking dreams, she was as brittle as a skeleton, with sunken eyes and teeth that had grown out long, like fingernails.

Jacob equipped himself with a lantern that we lit up good and gave plenty of oil. We handed him a torch we made from the campfire for his other hand, even though he wanted to hold a gun instead. It took some doing, but we convinced him there wasn't anything in there that would need shooting at, and besides—what if he fired off a shot in there? Wouldn't it bounce around? He might end up killing himself with his own itchy trigger finger.

He finally agreed to the torch and the lantern, mostly because he looked hard into the black room behind the slit in the hill, and he decided he wanted extra light more than he wanted to accidentally shoot himself in the face.

We congratulated him on his wisdom, and then we stood behind him—quite *far* behind him—while he worked himself up to walking inside.

I was wound tighter than an expensive watch.

I held my breath while he pushed himself forward and I could tell, watching him, that he was breathing just the opposite—fast and shallow. He was scared, and when he looked back over his shoulder I bet he was worried that he'd been tricked.

But he kept going. We were all watching him so he couldn't back out, not without losing face.

He had to step sideways to pass through the entrance. He led with the lantern; he paused there on the threshold, half in and half out of that other world. His neck craned forward, following the lantern. It slung back and forth from its handle, spilling runny yellow light into the interior.

With one more step he was wholly inside.

It was as if he'd been swallowed.

His lantern and torch bobbed merrily and cast their flames around, throwing reflections and lights from wall to wall. We watched him as best we could. Mostly, there was nothing to watch but a shadow skulking back and forth.

Nicodemus called out, "Pa, you all right in there?" But he didn't make a move to come any closer and see for himself.

Jacob called back, "Yeah."

"How's the air?" Uncle John asked.

"Smells like shit, but I ain't dying." Every word echoed, bounding around in the cavern, same as his lights. "Y'all get yourselves loaded up. Help me look around in here."

"What do you see?" I stalled.

He didn't answer at first. His lights wavered, and I thought maybe he was shining them around, trying to find something to tell me about.

Finally he said, "That Meshack asking?"

"Yeah."

"Then it's like you were saying—it splits up almost as soon as you get inside. And it looks like one way ends pretty quick, but the other one I can't tell. Get yourselves inside here." He stuck his head back out, and took a deep breath, and he shuddered. "Jesus. It stinks like hell, but there's only one direction we can rightly go, and nothing's done tried to eat me yet."

He grinned then, all proud of himself and glad he'd taken the challenge to go first. And he said, "Come on. There's no rigged-up traps or nothing, and I don't think it'll take long."

"All right," Carlson answered him, and everyone went around agreeing, but no one moved too fast.

"Uncle John," I whispered.

He didn't reply. He was staring hard at the cave entrance, and I didn't like it. He was staring at the cave like he'd been staring at the hillside before he spotted Boone's mark, like he saw something maybe no one else could see.

"Uncle John," I said again.

He turned to me and blinked.

While the other men started packing up their stuff, and while Jacob started whistling in the cave like a brave man, I asked my uncle, "If you see my sister in there, living or dead, would you tell me so?"

He sucked in a breath. "I don't believe I ever knew your sister, Meshack."

"That shouldn't make a difference. If there's a woman here, and if she's a ghost or if she's turned into something worse…that's surely her."

"Something worse?" he repeated after me. "What on earth do you mean by that?" There was real worry written on his face, and again I got that awful suspicion that he knew something I didn't.

"I don't know."

Everyone else was packed up and almost ready to head on forward, into the Pit. I tugged at Uncle John's arm and helped him shoulder a loaded-up pack. It wasn't too heavy, because we didn't intend to be down there for a week or anything. All of us were carrying extra oil, a few caving supplies like pick-axes and little shovels, a canteen, and some candles just in case.

"You sure?" he asked me.

"I'm not sure of anything," I admitted, and it was the truth. "Except for this bad feeling," I added. "I've got a real bad hurt in my stomach about this whole thing, and I don't like it—not any of it. Not at all."

And that was all I could confess. It was all I was willing to share, and anyway, the other fellows were waiting for us to hurry up.

Uncle John gave me a look, and for a second I couldn't figure out whether he wanted to give me a hug, or whether he wanted me to give *him* one. It made me uncomfortable, but I was almost grateful for it. I'd rather be embarrassed, than be scared so bad that I could hardly hold a pickaxe without it shaking.

"Let's go," I changed the subject. "They're waiting on us."

He nodded, and followed behind me. And one by one, in just about the same order we rode out, we filed into the Witch's Pit.

XII.

The Dead in the Pit

I DON'T KNOW WHAT I expected from the cave. I'd never been inside one before, and until that day I'd never seen a spirit before, either; but the cave surprised me more than the ghosts, I think. I'd expected darkness, and I'd expected the echoes of our voices and footsteps to patter back and forth across the walls. I'd anticipated the dampness, too.

But nothing could have prepared me for the sheer *stink* of the place.

From the outside we could detect it faintly, and to look at the ground around the entrance you'd think that nothing healthful could be emanating from within. To see all the dead grass and the swath of plants that had expired rather than grow in such proximity to the terrible smell...well...it made me worry for our lungs. Even if the air was not the strictest poison, it certainly could do us no good to breathe it for any duration.

Years ago, back when I was still there in the valley, a large raccoon somehow trapped itself in the outhouse hole and drowned in the sewage one summer. After two or three days of stewing in its fecal broth, the decaying raccoon's stench could have roughly compared to the rank air within the cave.

To put it in the mildest of all possible terms, it was *revolting*.

I didn't care what my fellow cavers thought of me. I retrieved my handkerchief and held it up to my nose, for all the slim assistance it provided. For a mere moment, I whiffed a faint memory of the lavender I kept in my drawers at home. The scent was overwhelmed almost before I could identify it.

I stuffed the square of fabric back into my pocket, which would have been tantamount to surrender if my efforts had not been so soundly and fairly defeated.

In places, the ceiling was quite low—and all across its expanse, as far as the lanterns could project, it was dripping with formations. Some were sharp and long, and they dangled down as delicate-looking as candle wax spilling away from a wick; but some were knobby and round, stone bubbles that glimmered wetly in the firelight.

We all held our heads low, and held our lights as high as we could.

Once we were inside, a great grumbling of swears broke the claustrophobic silence. Partly, the swearers were appalled by the odor, and partly they felt a nervous need to make some noise.

It was crushing, knowing the weight of a whole hill was held up by this dank, uneven ceiling—and we were walking beneath it. I could feel the heft of it, bearing down above me. And as silence fell between us once again, we held still and listened hard. I don't know what we were listening for; there was nothing to hear except for ourselves, and the occasional flicker and pop of a small flame bucking against a wick.

We could hear ourselves quite clearly, when we listened. Our breaths were low and measured, as if we all believed that there wasn't enough to breathe. Our hands tightened on our lights and our equipment, and the leather straps or metal holds creaked against our palms.

I cannot speak for the rest of them, but I could hear my own heart, too—pounding in my chest, bashing itself back and forth between my spine and my sternum. I could hear it madly pumping blood up through my temples.

And just when I thought it might make me crazy to stand there still, hearing my own body object to the surroundings, Titus said, "You think Boone ever came into this cave?"

He said it softly, but it was as loud as fireworks in the tiny black cathedral.

"I reckon he must've," Jacob answered. "Otherwise, why would he leave his mark beside it?"

General murmurs of agreement went all along the line.

Since the oppressiveness and fear was working on us all, Meshack kept us all moving. He suggested, "Let's spread out, just a little bit. I don't mean we should split up, but this room's pretty big, once you get looking at it. Let's make sure there's not some other passage out. Jacob, you said the room divides up."

"Yes, it does. Right here." He pointed at a wall that hung like a curtain made of melted rock. He indicated the left side of the curtain. "If you go that way, it dead-ends right quick. If you go the other way, it keeps on going. But now that all these lights are in here, I can see the place is bigger than I thought it was. There might be some other way—some other tunnel or something, leading someplace else."

"It's hard to tell, what with all the shadows," his son said. Nicodemus took a step away from the line and moved his torch, trying to see farther.

"Yeah, it is," Meshack agreed. "But we've got to look."

"We should look for signs of other men," I said. "If someone came to deliver a will or a deed, then he must've left tracks. Perhaps he left markings for us to follow."

"What kind of markings?" Carlson asked, but he sounded interested and not dismissive.

I shrugged and turned my shoulder to adjust the strap on my pack. "Chalk marks. Candle stubs. Letters or arrows written on the ceiling with smoke. Anything at all that says we're not the first to pass this way."

Titus added, "There might even be some sign left that Boone came here. Might find another mark of his, or something he might've dropped. There's no telling."

And with that added incentive, the men began to disperse.

We didn't stray far from one another, not more than a few yards. No one wanted to leave the sight of the group, and no one in the group wanted any one else to sneak away. It was a self-regulating system that kept us close.

We found it difficult to take our eyes off the floor in front of us, for it was terrifically uneven and difficult to navigate if we weren't paying the strictest attention. But we watched the ceiling and the walls, too, and at one point Nicodemus held up his lantern and said, "Look. Is that ours?"

On the ceiling, at a bare spot that was smoother than the rest of its surroundings, someone had smoked a straight line with a pointed end.

"It's an arrow," he added.

"It certainly looks like it," I nodded. "And since it indicates the direction we suspect to be deepest, we might assume that it's a message. People who explore caves mark their passage this way. Or it might have been left by whoever Heaster paid to deposit his will."

Meshack frowned. "I don't like it. I don't think Heaster would've left us any hints. He wasn't that kind."

No one argued, but Titus said, "Heaster wouldn't, sure. But I bet you a dollar he didn't come in here himself. Whoever he sent might've felt the need to be helpful. Or it might be the mark of somebody from years and years ago. Has anyone found any other way past this first split-up room?"

But we hadn't seen anything to indicate another passage.

"Then that's the way we have to go," Meshack said. He didn't sound happy about it.

There, again. At the edge of my vision, there he was.

A quivering shadow with light around the edges, there in the darkness. He was a silhouette with a face. And he was gone.

Then he stood in front of me, holding a candle.

No one else made any remark about him. The rest of the men were steeling themselves against the inevitable chore that would take us deeper and—unless we were mistaken—into the way where the atrocious stench was even greater. We were tracking it down, and we were creeping in closer to its source.

The ghost's candle was battered, a cut stump from a home-dipped wick. Its yellowish wax dribbled over his knuckles. His face was illuminated perfectly, almost brilliantly.

How was it that no one else could see him?

He was looking at me. Into the lines of his face was carved a hard determination. He was urging me on, urging *us* on. Whether or not he was the man who first smoked the pointing signal, he wished for us to follow it.

His mouth moved, and I heard a whisper that fluttered with disapproval, or unwillingness, or displeasure. I couldn't tell what.

You're not prepared, but you've got to try.

"Uncle John?"

I jumped. "Yes?"

Meshack was cloaked in darkness; his face was perfectly black because the bulk of the light was behind him and his own lantern was held in the direction of the passageway.

"What're you looking at?"

"Nothing," I said quickly, and it was true. The ghost was gone.

"You look awful," he said. He was trying to be quiet.

"I feel all right," I lied.

"Is something wrong?"

I wanted to tell him, but the room was too close and I would be overheard. "Nothing's wrong. I'm not accustomed to this, that's all. This close space, this darkness. It's unfamiliar. I'll adjust," I assured him.

He stared at me for a few seconds, probably guessing more than I'd told him, and then he said, "All right. Well, come on, then."

As we pushed ourselves forward in a small, disgruntled pack, the outside twilight of the cave entrance behind us was perfectly and briefly snuffed.

Then it blinked back into place.

I whirled around, and since I was following the rest of the men I had the best view of the white-gray portal. And the slit remained unbroken, if inadequate to give us any real illumination.

It was as if it were a window, and something had swiftly walked past.

I shoved my lantern forward, holding it out and wielding it like a weapon.

I saw nothing except for the empty cavern with its stone finger columns and posts, and its oozing, shining walls. But for an instant the smell was stronger. It blew past me in a gust that made my throat seize—and I couldn't stifle a tiny retch.

"Uncle John," Meshack said, and this time it wasn't a question. He could smell it too, so it wasn't a matter of my imagination or spirit intervention. Meshack had turned around, and placed his arm on my shoulder. "Come on, now. You don't want to get left behind in here."

In fact, I most certainly did *not* wish to be left behind. On the other hand, I did not wish to proceed even one inch deeper into the cave.

But I'd made my choice. I'd come this far. And I'd go as far as it was necessary to see this thing out.

I took another look around and saw no ghosts, nor any explanation for the stench. I followed after my nephew, whose hunched shoulders were stooping to pass beneath a low-hanging arch. The arch was a great marvel of nature; it was elaborately fanged with stalactites, the longest of which would have tapped against my elbow if I had not dodged it.

As I passed it, I reached out a hand and touched the thing. It was cold and slick. Even though I knew that only water coated it, I couldn't shake the feeling that I'd pressed my hand against something more gruesome.

I wiped my fingers against my pants.

Up front, Carlson held out an arm and said, "Wait a second. I think I found something."

It was too much to hope that he'd found the will, lying out and ready for us.

"What is it?" Jacob asked. He shoved his way forward and followed Carlson's light. "I don't see anything."

"That don't look like a handprint to you?"

"Where?" Jacob still wasn't seeing it.

Nicodemus came up with his light too, and yes, there it was—very faint. "I get it. Yeah, it sure looks like a handprint, made in mud or something."

"Mud," Meshack repeated, and an echo said it for him, a third time. "That don't look like mud to me," he said. He brought his face in close, then jerked back as if he'd been bitten. "I've never in all my life smelled mud like that. It smells like shit."

"Sure enough it smells like shit," Carlson affirmed, but I think he only meant the vernacular sense.

"No, I mean it smells like *shit*. Like a chicken coop on a hot day, except worse."

And while they hashed out the finer points of the terrible-smelling mud, a different noise reached my ears—bouncing from some wet wall or past another stone curtain. I heard it plain as day, and it was a clicking, sliding noise.

"Stop it!" I yelped, too fast and too loud to do anything but startle them into silence. When they were all quiet and looking at me, I said, "Don't you hear that? *Listen*."

"Hush up, you old lunatic," Nicodemus spit at the nearest column.

Carlson joined in. "It's not enough, you seeing things what ain't there. Now you're hearing things, too?"

I couldn't decide if I should be vindicated or terrified when the noise came again.

Slip, slip, scrape.

"There, you all heard—"

Meshack cut me off with a wave of his hand and a hasty *shhh*. Yes, he heard it. They all heard it.

"What the hell is that?" Carlson asked, but he had the good sense to drop his voice to barely more than a baby's sigh.

Shhh, Meshack insisted again, and Titus chimed in with a similar noise.

After ten or fifteen seconds of turning all our ears to the sound, Titus held his lantern up towards his face and mouthed, *Something heavy.*

Meshack agreed. *Coming closer*, he mouthed back.

I could barely see them trying to talk without making a sound, but every word they conveyed was a sharp pick in my stomach. Something heavy. Coming closer. If we held ourselves still and paid the utmost attention, we could hear it and yes, coming closer.

I didn't want to close my eyes; I didn't *dare* close them, despite the frightened and childish impulse that seized me.

Instead I concentrated and tried to imagine the shape and size of the thing that made the noise. The scrapes that accompanied the dragging noise had a rhythmic quality to them. It could've been footsteps, but they were too irregular—unless the creature walking was partly lame.

A glance around at the party told me the others were doing the same, trying to sort out what might make such an odd, intimidating noise.

"It might be nothing," Jacob said. His whisper was a shout in the watercolor blackness of the cave.

I wished to heaven that I could see the cave's entrance again, merely to know it was there and be reassured that there was an exit from this suffocating place with its seamless walls. But we were well past that, and no matter how hard I strained to see behind us, I saw nothing of the gray-white portal.

"What kind of nothing?" Nicodemus asked, and all the letters shook like they were being rattled in a box.

Someone was breathing hard and loud. The gasps took on a sharper, wheezing edge. I held my lantern up and towards the face of Carlson, who was squeezing his free hand along his ribcage. "Carlson?" I asked.

He waved as if to respond, but he couldn't answer.

By pure stubbornness he pulled himself together, despite the rising clamor of the heavy, dragging, closely approaching visitor—and make no mistake, we all believed that it was alive.

The thing that came our way was doing so with purpose. It was stalking forward, coming up from some distant hole or chamber; and with it, the stink came too, advancing ahead of it and warning, or promising, something terrible.

"We can't just sit here," Meshack said. He was shaking and tense. His arms were tight around the lantern he held, and I only then realized he'd retrieved one of those rock-picking axes. It perched firmly in his fist, held slightly aloft.

Titus was mirroring Meshack's stance, except that he had his revolver up instead of an axe. "Where do we go?"

"This is crazy!" Carlson finally squeaked. "It's just a noise. It's just a damn noise, and it can't hurt us or nothing. Whatever it is," he was barreling forward with his thoughts as if should he stop, he would not be able to begin again. "It's more afraid of us than we are of it, right? Isn't that what we tell the young'uns when—"

"Then why's it coming for us, if it's so scared?" Nicodemus snapped.

Carlson ignored Nicodemus and said to Titus, "Put down your goddamned gun, Mander."

"I'm not aiming it at you."

"I don't want to see it out no-how."

And with a ferocious click that had all the bang of a barking dog, Carlson had his own piece cocked.

"Not again!" I said in my full voice, and though I'm usually described as soft-spoken, I might have been screaming. I held out my arms and spoke above the one-two, one-two, slippery slide of the thing coming up close. "Not now, not here!"

Meshack tried to shove me aside, but I held my ground. "No," I swore. "Any one of you fires in this space, we'll all get killed, don't you understand? The bullets will bounce, they'll bounce and hit—"

I was interrupted by a call.

I'm at a loss to describe this call, except to say that it came at such a volume that I was reminded of standing on a riverboat a bit too close to the whistle. Although we felt no gust of wind to accompany it, the belching, grumbling croak breezed through our hair and rattled our clothes.

We were startled into perfect immobility, each one of us from youngest to oldest.

Carlson particularly looked pale, and his hand was over his heart—squeezing at the ribs and meat there.

And then, very quickly—so quickly that I must say it happened all at once—a slick orange shadow blinked behind Titus, and his lantern was extinguished in a swift, thunderous lurch.

Carlson screamed, and Nicodemus fired off one mad bullet that ricocheted with a series of stone-shearing pings and scrapes. Jacob was screaming too, but I couldn't tell why; and no one could see Titus. No one knew what had become of him.

He was there, and then a shadow that moved fast and thickly had covered him like a quilt, and then he was gone.

It had happened in less than a moment.

My body moved of its own accord, and I had no control over it at all. I flung myself backward, seeking some solid place of refuge or at least a spot from which I could defend myself from our unknown attacker. But it was not stone that I found, not at first. My backbone collided with something softer—though equally sturdy.

For a panic-stricken second I imagined a boulder covered with an eiderdown quilt.

The lantern in my hand burst backwards and I heard a tinkling crack as some part of it shattered against the cave wall.

Oil splashed, and a stray spark cast the overflow into a furious blast of spilling flame.

The whole room lit up into a collage of yellow, and copper, and black. Choppy silhouettes of frantic shapes cut across the light and although we had illumination to spare, it was impossible to see. It was impossible to think. It was impossible to do anything except grit my teeth and try to cover my head, because another piercing cry blasted out right in our midst, and the sound was purely astounding.

I turned my head and tried to examine the source but I saw nothing except a shapeless, lurching, wretched beast in a feather cloak—or that was the impression that reached my brain, at least. I couldn't imagine what else it could be; it was as if my memory was flipping through images in a picture book, desperate and grasping for something logical.

An Indian chief in an eagle headdress, turning and dancing around a fire.

A phoenix, engorged and rising.

It was on fire, and I wasn't sure why until I remembered the oil in my lantern. My hand was on fire too, and I hadn't noticed until the searing pain cut through my terror and confusion. I screamed and the flaming bird-beast screamed back.

A pair of wings, each the size of a carriage door, extended with such power that they might have been propelled by pistons or springs—and the nameless thing launched itself forward.

"Run!" I think it was Meshack's voice. "Run!" he said again, and then there was another round of gunfire but I do not know who began it and by then my ears were ringing so soundly that all I could hear was a whispering chime.

Bullets zipped around my head; one chinked against the stone wall beside me and tore at my sleeve, rending a perfect slice that—had it come any closer—would have drawn a fair amount of blood.

I was stunned. I was too stunned to move, though the men were moving around me. Someone was shouting for Titus, but I didn't see him. Someone was shouting for Pa, so that must've been Nicodemus; and someone shouted back, so that would have been Jacob.

Meshack grabbed my arm, and it stung because the bullet had clipped me close.

He propelled me forward, and he pushed me, shoved me, then pulled me onward—deeper into the cave—and I couldn't understand why. I even asked him, "Why?" and it came out like a pathetic shout. I hated the sound of my own voice, but I couldn't make it any stronger and I was increasingly certain that I had soiled myself with fright.

A hysterical thought of comfort alighted in my head.

At least no one will smell it.

Meshack wasn't answering me. He let my question linger in the air and as he drew me deeper into the darkness, I knew why. Behind us—behind me, for I was the last to follow—the awful flaming beast was blocking our only retreat to the open air.

XIII.

More than She Could Chew: Reflections from the Road, Daniel Boone, 1775

She knew where I was hiding, and we both knew it.

Little Heaster was gone, and his light was gone with him—so I was pretty sure she had the advantage over me. I could see it in her eyes when the moonlight caught them. They lit up, reflecting back at me in a pair of green-gold circles. Animals with eyes like that, they see real good when the light's low, because that's how God made them.

Unfortunate for me, I was not made in any such a fashion.

I couldn't see a thing, hardly, and what I *could* see I couldn't see with any real distinction. The whole world was one black shadow at the bottom of a bucket, at the bottom of a well.

I was breathing hard, but trying to slow it. I had to get hold of myself. I had to think.

I wanted to believe that my thinking could give me an advantage—a man can outthink a beast, and a man can make himself hold a branch on fire, even when he don't want to. But my fire was out, and I knew enough about the thing before me to know that she could think, too. She could trick. She could lie.

And she could see better than I could. Maybe she could hear better too.

But I listened for all I was worth.

I closed my eyes, since they weren't doing me any good anyway, and I opened my ears as best I could. At the edge of what I could hear, Heaster was getting away. Much closer, the creature was holding real still.

Only the hard crack of a splitting twig or the barest rustle of a too-close patch of leaves betrayed her.

At least I knew she hadn't followed him. At least she'd decided to stay and try to get a bite out of me. I was glad for that, even as I was shaking in my boots. Between me and Little Heaster, she'd have a harder time taking *me*.

I pressed my back against the tree and opened my eyes—and in those few seconds they'd adjusted, just a little. I still couldn't see much of anything, but there were shapes in the shadows now. The tall lines were trees. The quiet and shifty lump in the clearing was the beast that hunted me.

It was a terrible spot I was in.

I *knew* she knew where I was. But she wasn't coming for me. Not yet. She was keeping herself all silent; I couldn't even hear her feathers rustling, or her body twitching. The most that reached my ears was a loud dripping that sounded like soup being ladled slowly onto the ground from a very great height.

I could only pray that it was blood.

A clutch of leaves crunched under one huge foot. A second crunch came up closer to the tree I used to hide myself.

My thoughts were speeding in circles and I could not calm them. She was coming for me, and I had nowhere to hide. I shifted my grip on the axe, because that was all I was holding anymore. Everything else had been taken, or had fallen, or was simply lost. So I clung to that axe with both my hands and I prayed for guidance. I prayed for strength. I prayed for Little Heaster to make it back to camp unharmed.

Her feet were crashing against the earth, like she was lifting them up one at a time and testing them. She was stomping in place, but then she decided she'd had enough of that and she leaped—in just a couple of quick steps she'd be at my tree—and I had barely half a second to think about what to do.

When she was quiet, she was invisible.

When she was running, she was a terror of noise and sharp edges; and I did not need to see her lit up to know where she was coming from.

I turned and ran, and I ran myself smack into another tree within three steps. It hurt like crazy, but it was mostly just my shoulder and it could've been worse—it could've got me harder in the head, and it could've knocked me down. I didn't go down, but I staggered off to the side and she was right behind me.

She didn't expect me to cut so hard to the left, but then again, neither did I. Hitting the tree might've saved me from her, for just a few moments, so I kept staggering on around. I went behind her, back the way she'd come tearing at me. Her wing cast up a huge gust, a big wind that wasn't hard enough to blow me down, though it was hard enough to scare me silly. It felt like she was breathing right up against me, whispering into my ears. And all I could do was run, and run blind.

So I tried to think.

Was she hurt so bad that I could climb out of her reach? Ordinarily you don't think to climb a tree to escape something that flies, but I knew she was hurt. She was really hurt, even if she wasn't hurt as bad as she'd pretended.

I might try it, as a last resort.

Only as a last resort.

I ducked my head down, partly because it hurt so bad I had to, and partly because I was trying to shield it from the lower branches. And if I were to fall, I'd need to cover it anyway.

Of course, if I were to fall, that'd be pretty much the end of me.

She was moving lop-sided, having to turn herself to follow me between the closer trees. That gave me an idea.

I couldn't hardly see a thing, but if I could go farther back away from the Road, where the trees were smaller and closer together, I could feel my way along better—and she'd be even more hard-pressed to follow me. It was hard to remember which way to run, while I was trying to remember and trying not to kill myself against another tree trunk at the same time—and all the while, she was back behind me, huffing and puffing and trudging along so close, so fast, that I couldn't escape the smell of her.

Her beak snapped and I felt a tug and a jab at my back, to the right of my backbone. Hot pain scored down my ribs, right through the buckskin coat.

I didn't cry out. I didn't want her to think she'd hurt me.

She slowed me, though. She was biting down because she'd got a mouthful, and she was tugging, trying to pull me back by my coat. She was slashing at me, trying to snag the cut with her pointed face.

All I could do was keep moving. I was pretty sure I was leading her away from the Road, and I was pretty sure there was a gully that ran real deep and sharp alongside where we were cutting. I'd been through this land before, once or twice. I did my best to recall the way the ground was laid out. I did my best to take her far and deep, away from my Road, away from my men.

I didn't do a real great job of it, but if I must defend myself, it was awful dark and I was being chased by a monster.

I heard voices, somehow over the stomping rush of me running and her chasing. They were folks I recognized, voices I'd heard plenty before, and I had a moment of pure panic when I thought I'd led the damned creature right back into their midst.

Then I realized they were charging towards us. They were following the noise, and I'd told them not to come and help—I'd made them promise not to—but here they came, with fire and lanterns and guns, and axes, and God knew what else.

It made me mad, and that made me run faster, just from the rush of my anger. And by way of being fully truthful, I have to say that it made me feel a little glad, too. That creature was going to kill me if she could catch me. And if she could catch me, she'd keep on catching them, one by one, until she'd eaten the lot of us.

Well. I wasn't going to have any of that.

She couldn't have them. I wouldn't let her.

I stumbled.

The fall didn't take me down the way I expected. It took me down, and down, and farther. I'd found my gully.

She fell after me, spreading her wings and gliding—but not gliding very far. The gully was steeper on the far side. She must've been watching me not to notice. She must've been following so determined to catch me that it didn't occur to her to watch where she was going.

She hit the far wall of the gully and tumbled against it.

Her whole body objected to the tumbling. Her wings went one way, her talons were grabbing and clutching at roots that ripped and tore as they failed to hold her weight. I didn't have to see it. I could hear it. And it was going on right above me.

If I didn't move quick, she'd roll right back on top of me.

I moved quick. I tripped forward, uphill. I was hoping maybe the force of her rolling would keep her going on down, past me. It might have been a little advantage, but I was ready to grab it. I'd have done anything at all to keep her farther away, and keep her moving in some other direction.

When she landed she let out a squawk, and more wind, and something that squished.

She fell behind me, not by much. She didn't stay down, either. Slower now, and with a lot more effort by the sounds of things, she pulled herself up and started to crawl up, and out. I heard something strange when she flexed those wings; it wasn't just the sound of air being shoved by feathers, it was the sound of bones that weren't holding together very well. It was grinding and rough, like a wooden spoon stirring a bucket full of dry sand.

No matter how well she played possum, I didn't think she could pretend to be broken. And this time, I gathered it wasn't any pretending—because this time, she was making a retreat.

Behind me, I heard her struggling to rise.

Above me, at the gully's edge, I heard my men and I saw the light of their fires.

They bore down on her. One of them tripped right over me—didn't even see me. I understand that they were angry; she'd taken so many of us, and we were most of us friends.

And now they had her, and there were twenty of us and one of her, and she was all busted up.

She made it over the gully wall, mostly because my men had to climb down it and up the other side in order to chase her. I hauled my own self up too, because I wasn't going to let them go after her without me.

I didn't realize it until I started trying to follow them, but I'd gotten scuffed up pretty good, myself. I wouldn't know it until later, but I'd bashed my head open on that tree and I'd been bleeding all the while I was running from her.

That was all right. It didn't slow me down too bad.

When I caught up to them, I almost felt sorry for her.

They'd run out of ammunition by the time I reached them, since the guns would only go one round each, at best. The men had their axes swinging, though, and she was ducking out of the way, rolling back and forth, trying to dodge them.

She couldn't dodge them all.

One by one they struck her, sometimes individually, sometimes in packs. It was like watching wolves take apart a big deer, only better and worse at the same time.

The blows of the axes rained down—and in the dark, beside the gully, I heard the sounds of big bones cracking and wet feathers being beaten. By the light of the torches I saw her curling around herself, folding those wings forward, and I thought it was strange—because they were striking her everyplace. Most things think to cover their heads, and not their lower parts.

I had a flash of a thought. A memory of my wife, years before.

She was heavy with our third child, maybe a month or two away from delivering him. Out the front door, she was taking a pair of pails over to the barn to milk the cows, only she stopped just as soon as she got outside. And I heard her say, firm and insistent, "Daniel."

I got up from the place where I was sitting. Something about the way she said my name said trouble, only she didn't want to holler. I grabbed my gun and came out to stand beside her, and there was a cat—one of those big mountain cats, strong enough to take down a horse.

It wasn't a stone's throw away from her, but it was looking at her square in the face. But before I had time to raise the gun, the cat turned tail and disappeared into the woods. It was just as well. I don't care to shoot anything I can't eat, and I never heard of a cat that'd make good stew.

When I was sure the cat was gone, I looked down at my wife and she was whiter than a cloud. She was clutching her belly with one hand, and holding the other one out as if to ward the danger away.

The monster shuddered under the blows, and squealed and fumed as they hit her. I didn't try to call the men off, but for some reason, I didn't join them, either. I had as much reason as anyone to want her dead. I had as much right as the rest of them to put her down.

Maybe I even had more reason than they did. She'd killed some of them; but they were my responsibility. Maybe I was the one who should've passed that final judgment on her.

But I didn't. I'm not sure why, but I let them do it.

I let them hit her, and cut her, and bang their axes against her until she twitched and went still. Hell, I let them hit her for awhile even after that, because for one thing, they wanted to get it out—how mad they were because of how scared they'd been. And for another thing, me and Little Heaster had seen how she liked to play dead.

I was tired of her playing.

But I *did* wish it didn't take her so long to die.

Finally, she quit breathing. Finally, she was just a pile of pulp and feathers.

Maybe fifty paces away from the gully there was a cave. The whole of that territory is pocked with them, and if you think about it too hard, it'll make you feel uneasy about walking around, all that hollow earth underneath you.

The cave I knew was hardly a hole in the ground, but I'd seen it before when I'd been passing through. I didn't care much about poking around in caves, because I don't like the damp and I don't like the crowded feeling they give me. I don't mind the dark, but I don't like being stuck someplace without any windows.

Between us, we half rolled, half carried the creature's stinking carcass to the cave's mouth, and we kicked her inside.

We could've left her lying out in the air to rot, I guess, but we didn't want to smell her. It felt more right—more *final*, I guess I mean to say—to put her into the ground, even if we weren't burying her. And we needed real bad to be done with her.

Anyway, we had a Road to finish.

XIV.

Down Below the Bottom

UNCLE JOHN FROZE LIKE a scared raccoon, when he backed up and ran right into that thing—that whatever-it-was. I saw where he was going and I wanted to stop him, but it was like he couldn't hear me. There was so much noise, after the guns went off, in that tiny tight space. Maybe it hurt his ears. It hurt mine, too.

His shoulder knocked against the creature and he took a quick gasp like he was going to start hollering.

He didn't yell. Nothing came out but a wheeze and a cough, because he was scared so bad he couldn't move at all, not even to breathe. And bless him, he couldn't even see what he'd smacked up against. At first I thought he was being stupid, not having the good sense to turn around and take a look; but then I figured it was just as well.

If he'd looked over his shoulder, he might've turned to stone or salt.

But Jesus, when his lantern spilled the oil—and God Almighty, when the flame licked it up and the light went reaching up to the cave's ceiling, it was like that beast was some holy thing.

My wife's mother gave her a Bible, one of those old books half as big as a suitcase. Inside it there are pages with paintings on them, showing scenes from the stories. Somewhere towards the back there's a page from one of the prophet's dreams about the end of the world.

It's a picture of wings burned up by the fires of hell, but still lit up with the glory they once knew in Heaven. It's a fallen angel, I guess—created beautiful and bright, then twisted and scalded by Satan.

As the oil burned around it the monster began to shake, trying to fling the flaming droplets away from its body. It scattered the oil. It sprayed the sparkling stuff against the walls where it glowed and dripped, and sizzled against the dampness there.

Behind me, the Manders and my cousin Carlson were scrambling for an exit, but it became real clear real fast that there wasn't any exit except the way we'd come in—and with that monster standing there, squawking and raging and ready to kill, we surely couldn't go back.

There was no way out but down.

I was scared as hell by the prospect of going even deeper. I mean, Christ—weren't we already at the bottom? But there wasn't any time to think on it. We only had a moment there, while the beast was all sparked up and thrashing, to decide which way we were going to go.

Uncle John was pinned by it, almost. He was up against the cave wall beside the passage that had led us this far. Looking back on it now, maybe I should've shoved him past the monster. We maybe could have made it out, just the two of us. We maybe could've burst past it and back out into the main room, out into the open air.

But there was just no time.

I could only move in jerks, letting my arms and legs do the thinking for me—because they did it faster.

I grabbed Uncle John by the shoulder and he let out a yelp. I didn't realize then that he'd been nicked by someone's gunshot and he was bleeding. In that small cave room with the one way coming in and the one way going out, so much was happening that it was impossible to even *see* everything at once, much less notice it.

So I took Uncle John and I squeezed his arm real tight, and I yanked him away from the entrance hole and away from that flaming great bird-monster with the huge wings that bucked and jerked.

I pulled him forward, away from the wall. He stumbled after me, not fighting me exactly, but not helping me much, either.

I knew he was only scared and stunned. Yeah, well. We were all scared and stunned, but he was the only one who wasn't running of his own accord.

I drew him back, farther into the darkness except that it wasn't as dark as it might've been because the others had gone ahead of us, and they had lights. They were charging on back, not picking any real direction except "away, and as fast as we can."

I followed them, trying to track the wild swinging of their lights as they held them up, trying to see and trying to run.

Since I had Uncle John's arm in one hand, I'd had to stuff my pickaxe down into my belt in order to hold both him and my own lantern. His was destroyed against the cave wall, or against the monster, I don't know which. I saw it happen, and I still couldn't tell you exactly how it all took place.

Without me, he'd be in the dark, and I was in the semi-dark as long as I stuck with him, because one little flame in a hurricane glass can only do so much underground, and it took me a minute or two of staggering to catch up to the other men.

Those moments between the monster and the Manders are hard to recall, except in pieces. I remember seeing the flames bound off the wet stone shapes; and I remember seeing blood from somewhere, from something, smeared across one of the skinny, pointed columns that dangled from the ceiling.

As far as I could tell, no one had ever cut a road through that cave. No one ever cleaned a path or evened out the walkways, such as they were. A cave is cut by water, or that's how I understand it, and water doesn't cut very cleanly. There weren't any real paths to speak of. There weren't any handrails or lamps set into the walls.

I thought, *This must be what it's like to be an ant in a hill. Always crawling and climbing, always ducking and scrambling, and there are never any windows.*

I banged my legs up real good, and Uncle John did even worse to himself. He tripped over the floor and landed hands-down on the sharp stone spikes that came up from the floor. He let out a sharp, high-pitched squeal with an edge of pain that was high and hard, and more specific than plain old fear.

"Come on," I told him, tugging him forward. The others were getting ahead of us, and I couldn't see what was behind us. "Come on."

"Yes," he said back to me. I didn't look behind to see how bad he was hurt, and he didn't say anything about it. He only made a better effort to move his own legs without me dragging him.

I don't know how far we went, or how long it took us to catch up to everyone else. We didn't catch them all at once. They were starting to separate from the one big clump of stomping feet and swinging lanterns. They were sorting by who had the most energy, and who was least hurt, and who was most scared.

Carlson was straggling back. I almost kicked him for not seeing him.

He was panting and coughing, all doubled over his lantern and clutching his chest. "My heart," he said.

When I'd stopped so sudden over Carlson, Uncle John had almost crashed up against me. He sorted himself out and said to our cousin, "Just calm down, now. Don't get too excited, it'll only make it worse."

And he said it so serious that I couldn't tell him how dumb it sounded. Just calm down? Don't get too excited? Not five minutes before he'd been so scared he'd pissed himself, and here he was telling another man to pull himself together. Like everything else, I suppose it's easier to say than do. I know he was only trying to help, but I almost had to laugh at him.

He bent down to Carlson and wrapped one arm underneath him, lifting the other man up to his feet. I had to give him credit. My uncle was stronger than he looked underneath that too-nice suit.

And then I thought, *Well, he's one of us after all, ain't he?*

On his way up to a standing position, Uncle John picked up Carlson's lantern, too. Carlson didn't look like he could hold it anyhow.

Something loud snapped in the tunnel back the way we came. I didn't have to see it to guess what it was—one of them big columns being broke as easy as stepping on a twig. There was a clattering crash, and I didn't see any light back there so the fire must be out.

A faint gust of air pushed past us, all around, like the cave itself was breathing.

We smelled the chicken-coop-shit again, and there was something else too. It was a smell of burning hair, or feathers. I thought the place couldn't have stunk any worse, but I'd been wrong.

I was sure the hair was peeling right off my arms.

"It smells…like…" Carlson was talking slow, squeezing out a word or two between breaths.

"Like shit, yeah," I told him. "No time to admire it. We've got to keep moving."

"How do we slow it down?" Uncle John asked. By then, he was keeping pace with me pretty good, even though Carlson must've been practically dead weight.

"Why would I know?" I groused back at him. I didn't mean to be cross, but he'd seen exactly the same thing as I had, and he knew exactly as much about it as I did—so we both knew exactly the same: *nothing*.

"It's *coming*." He said it all urgent but low.

"We're *going*," I told him.

And then I didn't know *where* we were going, because Carlson had stopped at a fork where the passage split into three directions. I didn't want to be in charge; I didn't want to lead anybody anywhere, even if that meant I had two warm bodies between me and the thing that was trying to eat me.

"There," Uncle John pointed.

And I saw, just for a twinkle, a spark of light disappearing behind a rocky wall down the far left fork.

"All right, all right." I knocked my knees against the tough, spoke-scattered floor and wished to God for a straight stretch to run.

"Watch out for that," I twitched the lantern at a spot in the floor where the ground opened up like a pothole in a city street.

Uncle John stepped around it. He carried Carlson over it, hauling him past it and over to the other side. I put out a hand and pulled my uncle over. He was sweating and bleeding; his one hand was wholly covered and running with blood, and the scratch on his shoulder from the wayward bullet was oozing, too.

But he wasn't bitching, and he wasn't screaming. He'd got himself sorted out enough to act like a man.

He was even thinking straight, for all the good it did us. There was no sense in keeping too quiet—it wasn't like the thing couldn't hear us, anyway—so I didn't stop him. I let him ramble in case he was going to blurt out something useful.

He said, "We have to find a safe place, or a safer place. We have to find a spot we can defend. We can't just run forever, and if we don't pay attention—*pay attention*!" he said louder, trying to make me see that I was about to hit my head on a rock curtain that swung out into the way.

I nodded my head under it and kept going.

"And if we don't pay attention, we're going to get lost. Are you counting the turns?"

"Counting the…what?" I didn't know what he meant.

"Counting the turns. We came inside and went straight, then to the left, and now we've taken the leftmost way again."

"We're circling."

"No," he said. Carlson coughed again and I dared a glance back to see that he was slumping and almost helpless. Uncle John added, "We're *spiraling*."

I got what he meant. We were going down. "It's going to trap us down here."

"It's going to try."

Up ahead we heard a clamor and a yell. "Stay back!" somebody ordered, and I heard the cocking of more guns being brought to the ready.

"It's us!" I announced. "Just us! It's behind us!"

I didn't slow down or stop, I just came on forward without my gun and without my axe up. I wanted them to see that we were dragging a body with us, and that we weren't trying to start anything.

We caught up to them then, Jacob and Nicodemus who were huddled with their guns drawn behind a big column. But there was a vast, empty hole behind them. They hadn't backed themselves up against anything, not even a corner.

"Where's Titus?" I asked.

They rose up from behind their column and weren't listening to me; they were listening to the charging, crashing, incoming monster. I couldn't tell how much of a lead we had, but I could bet it wasn't much.

Jacob frowned and said, "He ain't with you?"

"He ain't with us," I responded. He might've thought Carlson was Titus, since his face was hanging down against his chest. I brought the light around as Uncle John caught up and I saw how red his cheeks were from all the running.

"We got to keep moving anyhow," Nicodemus said.

I didn't want to keep moving, not just yet. I wanted to know about Titus. "Where'd he go? Did you see him? Did he get split up from you?"

"I don't know," Nicodemus swore.

I wanted to press him for details but it was getting louder, and the echo kicked the sound all over the place.

Uncle John answered through the noise and distraction. He said, "Back at the beginning, when the…when that creature first appeared. Titus fell backwards, or maybe it grabbed him."

I turned around fast and I stared him down, trying to make out if he was telling the truth, or telling us what he thought we ought to hear to keep us moving. But he wasn't looking at me when he talked. He was looking somewhere else, off in the distance—into the darkness behind the column.

"Uncle John?"

"We have to keep moving. But not that way," he said, which stopped Nicodemus in his tracks. He was about to go tearing back even farther behind that column, back into a spot so vast and so black that the edges of our lantern-lights combined couldn't suss out its depths.

"Not that way," John said again. He sounded calm, but a little confused for someone who was giving orders. "There's…back there. The other way. There's another…here." He handed Carlson to me, like I knew what to do with him. "Take him, just for a minute. Let me look."

"We haven't got any minutes!" Nicodemus was shrill.

"We can't keep up this retreat!" John shrieked back at him. "We can't let it trap us down and—"

And I don't know what the rest of it was going to sound like, because he got interrupted by a fearsome shriek. It was close.

No, it was right on top of us.

It leaped out of the wide black wall of nothing and bounced—I swear, it bounced—up over the small pit in the floor and almost into our midst, except we were already scrambling to get out of the way.

"Not that way!" John shouted, and again and again over the scuffle. "Not that way!"

Nicodemus was shouting back and his gun was going off. The report was so loud that the whole cavern shook, and the soft bits inside my ears were trembling. I wanted to cover them and duck my head but there was too much danger.

"I ain't taking orders from no goddamned—"

And he fired again, and I wished I had my own gun handier so I could shoot him. That wasn't too nice or fair of me, but there you have it. A horrible monster was trying to catch and kill us, and that goddamned idiot was worried about who should give directions.

Uncle John was moving, trying to wrangle the Manders into staying away from one particular corner of darkness. I was looking for someplace to drop Carlson, who was hanging off my arm—but then he pushed himself off me, letting go and falling forward. He was holding a pickaxe and I wondered where he got it, until I noticed that mine wasn't hanging on my belt anymore.

Carlson lifted one of his lanky arms and as the creature reared up—like a horse that don't want a bridle—my cousin chucked the axe. It spun head over handle in a perfect straight line, and it dug itself in right into the dead middle of the thing's forehead.

Anything else would've dropped like a stone.

That creature did not drop.

It stopped, and swayed, and then it swung its head and knocked the axe against a stone pillar; the axe fell down to the bumpy ground with a terrible loud clatter.

It stopped, but it didn't fall down.

We stared at it—wondering if we'd hurt it so bad that it'd die. Nicodemus emptied the last of his bullets against the creature's body but as far as I could tell, it didn't hardly notice.

I'd been counting his bullets and I was glad he was finished. I didn't think I could stand listening to another round shot off inside that closed-up place.

We all stood still, not sure if we should run or attack. And then, outside the edge of the bubble our lanterns cast, beyond the safely seen places where our lights could reach, something else stirred.

The other men were watching the injured beast thrash and recoil. I kept my eyes on the movement, which was going on so close, but so deeply shadowed that I had to glare in order to see it. I reached behind my shoulder and pulled my rifle down. I aimed it and held it steady.

Uncle John saw what I was doing.

He kept his voice low, but he knew everyone could hear him. "We're not finished. We're going to have to run. Nicodemus? Don't go back that way. There's trouble back that way."

"What's going on?" he asked. He was starting to relax, watching the monster start to shudder on its feet. "What are you going on about?"

And then Uncle John said, all matter-of-fact and quiet, "We're not alone here."

"Titus!" Jacob shouted. "Titus, you hear us?"

I almost brought the rifle around to point it at him, but I held my stance. "Shut up!" I hissed instead.

"Titus!" He hollered it again.

Uncle John put his hand on my shoulder, leaving a bloody smudge there. He whispered, "Titus is dead."

"How do you know?"

"Because I saw him," my uncle said.

I thought the way he put it was kind of weird. I didn't say anything about it, at the time. As my wife might say, 'my attention was elsewhere.'

Jacob sneered and said, "You're full of shit, you dumb son of a bitch. *Titus*!"

And all of a sudden—just like that, with a mad, pounding rush of muscle and feathers—some spot I hadn't seen burst to life. Practically behind me, another beast blasted out of the unlit edges and clamped its beakish mouth down towards Jacob's throat.

The curved, sharp edges of the bird-looking maw drove down fast, and if it'd landed, it would've snipped through muscles like a pair of scissors. But Jacob's son jerked him out of the way and they tumbled back together away from the new threat.

Carlson bellowed and took shuffling steps towards Uncle John, not to attack him I don't think, but to follow him. Under ordinary circumstances I don't believe Carlson would've followed him to an outhouse, much less anywhere in an ink-black cave that harbored creatures that were happy to kill.

But Uncle John sounded like he knew what he was doing, sort of, so we all began to back up, as fast as we could and not with any grace at all, in the direction that my uncle was leading.

It was a chaos, a nightmare, and a pathetic scramble of men holding guns and waving picks, and swinging lanterns.

And we were climbing, not toppling. Uncle John was taking us up, but everyone knew that up might not mean out right away—

not with a whole huge hill above us; and behind us, not quite below us yet, there were more lumbering shoulders covered with filth-shining feathers.

Carlson fell and I picked him up with the arm that was holding my rifle by its stock. I was under him again, and he was moving better with me now, getting used to it. We still weren't moving none too quick.

Then, for no reason I could understand, he started to resist. He was pulling back away from me like he wanted me to let him go, so I said, "You damn fool, what are you doing?" And then I looked to see what was keeping him.

He wasn't being ornery.

When I twisted my neck I could see his face, and it was so white with fear that even in the half-light of our wavering lanterns I could see he was giving up the ghost, right there.

His mouth was open; he was trying to shout or tell me something, but no words were coming and his feet weren't dragging—they were being dragged.

I had no way to bring the gun up from under him. I couldn't have fired without killing him, and maybe the kick of it would knock the gun away too, and I'd lose that as well. So I tried to pull him away, like some crazy tug-of-war.

While the rest of the men scurried up—not straight up, but leaning and lurching up an incline of jagged and wet stone—I was stuck, and being left behind in that nightmare place.

Carlson didn't have any strength to hang on, and the night underground was crawling with motion, and I couldn't make any sense of any of it but so help me, I was not going to die there alone, guarding a man whose heart was already half gone.

So I let go.

I didn't hear what happened next. I couldn't hear anything except my own heart pounding like an Indian's drum, and my own feet slipping and scraping, struggling for purchase on the unfriendly floor at the bottom of the earth.

XV.

The Dead and the Damned

MESHACK SCRAMBLED TO CATCH up with us. He was alone.

"Carlson?" I asked.

"Dead," he answered.

Behind and below us, I heard the most terrible wet snapping noises, and the sound of thick things being torn. I heard the clatter of beaked jaws clicking together. I didn't ask anymore about Carlson.

Instead, I asked, "How many of those *things* did you see?"

He said, "Three for sure. Three at least, including the one we hurt. Probably more."

"We didn't kill it?" I said "we" as if I'd had anything to do with it. Among them, I was the only man unarmed, and I knew that I was the least helpful from a defensive standpoint.

"Doubt it," he replied. "But it might not follow us anymore. You said Titus was dead." It wasn't a question this time.

"He's dead," I confirmed. "He was the first one we lost."

"And now Carlson. So it's the four of us, then. Two Manders, and two Coys."

I shook my head. "No, not divided that way. There's four of us, that's all. No us-and-them down here."

"Easy for us to say. You convince *them* we're all together, and maybe I'll reconsider my math."

I slipped, and grabbed at a pointed bit of stone out of reflex—trying to steady myself; but I took it with my injured hand, and the pain was absolutely blinding. In my other fist I held another man's lantern. Was it Carlson's? I couldn't recall. I remembered picking it up, but nothing else about how I'd come to hold it. It was running low on oil, either from being sloshed or simply from being burned.

"Meshack, how many candles do you have?"

"Some," he said, which was a less precise answer than I would have preferred. "Hey Manders!" he called ahead. "Y'all still got some candles, too? Or more oil?"

The huffing, puffing, and panting up ahead slowed and Nicodemus said over his shoulder, "You running low?"

"Naw, just asking."

"Gentlemen," I begged. "*Quiet*."

"Like they don't know where we're at," Jacob complained.

He was right, of course. They were swarming up behind us, the three monsters or however many. They'd been distracted by Carlson's body but it wouldn't hold them long.

We caught up to the Manders, who were slowing down from exhaustion—while we were moving faster because we'd been bringing up the rear, and we had the things on our heels.

"Where are we going now?" Nicodemus asked. "Where are we trying to get to?"

"I don't know," I said.

"You're the one who pushed us this way!"

"I know!"

"But you don't know what to do? Then why'd you make such a fuss? You ain't never been here before neither," Jacob fumed.

The way widened, and Meshack and I moved side-by-side, up to overtake the Manders. "Because," I told Jacob when I was right beside his face. "We can't keep going down. We can't let them bury us here. We're going to have to outthink these things, or they're going to pick us off one at a time, until there's no one left to shoot or shout!"

"What happens if we get stuck? Up don't mean out," Jacob argued. "We can get ourselves penned up against the ceiling just as easy as the basement floor."

"You're right," I said. "But...I had a feeling."

"A feeling?"

"Yes." I also had a vision, but I couldn't tell him that part. It wasn't a vision like a dream, like a prophet's guide or mystical knowledge. It was a vision of a man in a buckskin suit; and he was holding an axe over his shoulder and holding up his arm, as if to block that downward way.

If the spirit was Daniel Boone—and I was choosing to believe as much—then I had to assume he meant us no harm.

"Boone didn't die in these caves," I breathed. I hadn't meant to say it out loud.

Meshack asked, "What?"

"I was only thinking aloud. Boone didn't die in these caves. He died an old man in his bed. He made it past this cave. We can make it out." That's what I said, but it was thinking on my feet. What I meant was, *Boone didn't die here—but he's come back. He knows what's down here, and maybe he knows how to beat it.*

Boone hadn't wanted us to keep going down. He was trying to send us up.

If Meshack knew I was lying, he kept that information to himself.

Our passage narrowed again, immediately and harshly. On the other side of the tight spot there was another opening, and another set of forked paths. I counted four. Jacob pointed out a smaller route down in the floor that seemed to lead back too, so that made five alternatives, none of which looked better than the rest.

"Oh spirits," I said, trying to make it sound like a curse—but it was actually a prayer.

My devotion and desperation must have shined through the short exclamation, because Jacob was unconvinced. "Don't you start none of that funny shit," he commanded.

"I'm only asking for help. At the moment, I think you'd agree, we could use any assistance we can summon."

"Then pray to Jesus or something!" he threw his hands up, and the glow of his lantern kicked and wobbled. He was running low on oil, too. We were going to need those candles.

"You first," I mumbled. I was scanning the narrow, dark premises, seeking some hint of divine intervention that was more easily interpreted than a burning bush or heavenly dove.

"Maybe we ought to," his son said slowly. "Maybe we ought to close our eyes and try it."

"Go on then, cast your own little spells and pretend they're something else, if that's how you want to handle this," I said, and I did my best to keep the contempt out of my words, but I'm sure that I failed at least in part. "Do whatever you want, but for the love of whoever you worship, *don't close your eyes*."

Meshack was surprisingly silent during our small argument. He was watching it, and watching the walls, and watching the way behind us.

Finally he said, "They're still coming."

"And we're still sitting here!" Nicodemus all but shouted. He blinked frantically back and forth between the options and then said, "Maybe we should split up? Go different directions? They can't chase us all down, can they?"

Meshack said, "They can if there's more of them than there are of us."

"You think there are?" Nicodemus squeaked.

"I'm pretty sure of it, now that you ask." He looked up at the stone curtains above and around us, and he frowned back at the way we'd come. "We can't just keep running like this."

Jacob glanced unhappily down at his lantern with its dwindling light. "What would you recommend then, farmer boy?"

"It's like my uncle's been saying, we've got to get up and get out. Or, if that don't work, we're going to have to find a place to hole up and hold them off."

"How many bullets you think we brought?" Nicodemus asked, as if he couldn't believe anyone would be dumb enough to suggest a stand-off.

Meshack didn't pay any attention to the young man's tone. "Between what we've got left and the pickaxes, we might can hold them long enough to figure something out. I'm not talking about making a stand—I mean we need to buy ourselves some time." He turned to me, then. And there was a look on his face that was almost desperate. "You're sure Titus is dead?" he asked.

"Yes," I swore. "I'm sorry. I know you were friends, but he's gone. I saw it happen."

"You saw it happen," he repeated. He wasn't questioning me; he was tasting the words and finding them bitter.

A louder clamor and rustle popped and echoed up behind us. "Meshack, gentlemen," I insisted. "We *must* do something!"

"Maybe we should go back," Meshack said. "Go back to that little bottleneck there, and hold it like a fortress."

I thought it was more likely he wanted to go back in case Titus had somehow fought his way through, but I didn't interrupt him about it. I understood that he hadn't seen it happen, so he couldn't have known it the way I knew it.

There wasn't any time to take such a course. The creatures were rising up, swarming their way through the bottleneck; we heard something stone and slippery crack and break, and we heard frenetic, scuttling claws climbing fast behind us.

"Which way?" Nicodemus demanded, and I didn't know what to tell him.

"That way," Meshack said quickly. There was no reason to argue. No one had any better ideas, so I clamored up the way he indicated. It was farther up and not down, so I approved. But Jacob's earlier objection was rambling through my mind, and I thought that it would be a horrible way to drown—pinned against the ceiling by a rising tide of monstrous great bodies.

There was no right thing to do.

There was no right choice.

So I followed Meshack's directions, and as I watched my lantern flame flicker and threaten to gutter, I stole a quick peek back at the source.

Meshack was bringing up the rear this time. He was charging towards me, his own lantern jerking back and forth as he pumped his legs as fast as they'd come up the broken and unpredictable terrain. "Go!" he shouted at me, and I tried, but I was transfixed by the action at the bottleneck.

In the few seconds between Meshack's warning and his rough collision that carried me back, and up, and away from the scene... I saw Boone once more.

He was there. He hadn't left us to die harried and lost in the darkness. The spirit was standing with the shadow of a great, glistening-sharp axe in his hands. His legs were spread, feet planted apart so the apparition of his body blocked the opening—and he waved that axe and I swear, the beasts were hesitating. They crawled over one another to back away from him, and to keep from touching him.

His ectoplasmic axe glistened a sharp and forbidding warning. He whipped it over his head, and back and forth, and down low, and high.

They could see him.

And he cut his passage with the blade, and they did not push at him—even though they could have surely leaped right through him.

"They can see him!" I gasped as Meshack barreled into me. The young farmer clapped one of his long arms around my chest and lurched us both through the next passageway. I didn't struggle against him; I was only so shocked and bewildered by the sight of it.

I knew that beasts might see a spirit more easily than mankind, but I couldn't shake the impression that they didn't only see him, they *recognized* him.

It was a silly thing to think; it was a preposterous detail to assume, but I did—and as Meshack half shoved, half led me away, I silently

M. Geyer

prayed a universal thanks for the assistance, because it had come to us exactly as I asked. Then, realizing that I was squandering the lead we were being offered, I turned around in Meshack's prodding grasp and began to run alongside him.

We hadn't gone more than a few yards when a scream up ahead announced more trouble.

There was nowhere for us to go—and we'd built up enough speed that we couldn't help but run headlong into it.

It was another one of the hideous bird-like monsters—so we had not three, not four, but at least five of them to contend with—and it had Nicodemus locked underneath one of its massive talons.

He rolled and twitched, and he swung his lantern up against the creature's leg. It broke, and it caught—just like it had in that first chamber, back at the beginning. This one screamed too, another awful shriek that shook the pretty stone pillars and peaks in the ceiling above us. It spun around, flapping its massive wings and beating out most of the flame.

But it'd been distracted long enough for Jacob to go in low and grab his son. Meshack joined him, seizing one of the man's legs and yanking him free of the beast that was stomping, crashing, spinning in the tight space.

The whole room reeked of smoke and burning feathers, and it was hard to see for all the blackened air—and now we were one light less than before.

It almost gave me a panic to think of it—yes, a worse panic than the flailing creature with the snapping beak that chomped at the air with a force that would have broken furniture. We were in a new chamber now, a smaller chamber that couldn't have held even one more body for all the cramped space. Nicodemus was hurt, but for the moment he was more frightened than injured and he hustled up and over a short ledge with his father's help.

Nicodemus had dropped his gun. It was lying on the ground, half aimed up from a crack where it had settled.

Meshack had his rifle drawn, but when he jerked the trigger something jammed and the long, loud machine didn't fire.

I was almost relieved. I was beginning to fear for the integrity of our space. One more terrible noise and the whole place might come crashing down, and then wouldn't we be buried!

But the beast's neck stretched, faster and harder than any rubber band and it clamped that scissor-blade beak down on Meshack's rifle. I was astonished when the metal barrel didn't snip clean away, but it only bent sharply with the shape of the thing's boney mouth. Meshack held the butt end of the gun and tried to wrestle it away but the bird-beast wasn't finished with him yet. It kicked up an enormous foot, and my lamplight glittered against the enormous claws that tipped the end of each long toe.

Meshack almost folded himself in half as he ducked away. The claw sliced him, but barely, and cleanly, and across the torso. The scratch went from his collarbone to his lower left rib and it went red within the blink of a moment.

It could've been worse, I frantically assured myself. It could've been so much worse! Mere inches lower and deeper, and he'd be holding his own entrails. But it was a fleeting thought, and I gave it no time to take hold or inspire any comfort.

Meshack staggered back against the short ledge that the Manders had scaled as they fled. I could hear them, kicking and fighting against the very rock itself as they strained to haul themselves up, or back, or down, or however the corridor kinked and ran beyond the spot where we could see it.

And there was Nicodemus's gun on the ground.

I had never fired a gun in my life. No, not even when I was young and I lived in the valley. I've always been terrified of them. The noise, the power, the devastation—but there was my nephew, and he had just assisted in the rescue of another man…a man who had then deserted us both.

I seized the gun and I aimed it at the creature. It turned to look me in the face. It saw a skinny old man with a dwindling lantern in one hand and a firearm held awkwardly in the other.

Meshack had pulled himself upright and was pushing his feet against the uneven wall, reaching up and back for the ledge. "John," he wheezed. "*Don't.*"

He must've thought the same thing I did. Too close to shoot. Too many rounded walls, boxing us all close and together. The seared scrape on my arm stung and reminded me of the way a bullet might bounce, and I was afraid, but I was also afraid of the smashed-moon face that glared with tufted eyebrows.

I dashed for the ledge and leaped up it, nearly throwing my lantern and extinguishing it in the process, but Meshack caught the light by its wire handle and caught me by the arm. He helped lift me up and pull me through.

He grabbed the gun out of my hand and pulled the hammer back—which I had not thought to do, for I knew so little about the way these things operate.

Then, with both of us up and the creature's face biting into the opening where we'd squeezed ourselves, he pulled the trigger. Twice he hit the thing in the face, once in the mouth, I think. It blew back away from us, now sporting a splintered hole in its beak and a badly burned patch on the side of its eye.

Meshack pulled the trigger again but either the gun failed or I did not hear it because I couldn't hear anything, anymore. The sound of the shot was too much for my already too-much abused ears; something was broken inside them, or inside the left one at any rate.

A stabbing pain shrieked through my skull but there was nothing to do but run, run, climb, and run. It was almost easier when I couldn't hear, and I couldn't know the maddening distraction of the furious pursuit at our heels.

Meshack didn't have to pull me anymore. I labored along beside him, scuffling through the wet and slippery stink of the corridor that was, in some places, almost too narrow to accommodate either one of us.

We pushed our way through, and up, and past.

In the tangling rush of our escape, I passed my nephew in the corridor. That's how we accomplished our retreat, leapfrogging one another at the side, trying to push on up and past, and knowing (although I could not detect it) that the cacophony of evil bird voices echoed down below.

We were walking with our hands as much as our feet, and my hand was a furnace of pain and remarkable, blessed numbness in spots that made me think perhaps I'd damaged something irreparably. For one berzerk moment, I thought perhaps I'd lost the hand altogether, and there was so much disaster chasing from every corner that I'd simply failed to notice.

But then I dropped my knuckles to steady myself, and I did not find the textured stone beneath it.

I felt leather.

I stopped abruptly. Meshack ran into me from behind. I was holding the light; we'd traded for whoever was in front. He didn't see me, I shouldn't think—though how I hadn't seen the dead man is a question I cannot answer.

But there he was, or rather, there was part of him.

There were legs, both of which had been gnawed down to bone at the thigh. There were ribs, too, scattered someplace. All of it was gruesomely fresh, and it must've occurred within seconds! What kind of creature—or, I shuddered to think, what appalling number of them—could strip a man down to loose parts in such a brief span of moments?

"Who is it?" Meshack asked. He crawled over to be next to me and repeated himself loudly into my ear, for I hadn't heard him the first time. A whole choir of bells was banging behind my eyes, rattling my senses even worse than they were already shaken.

"I can't tell," I confessed.

"Me neither," he said, and something in his voice cracked.

Could this be Titus? Or one of the other Manders? Or someone altogether different, whose presence in the cave had gone unknown to us?

I cocked my head to listen to him with my right ear, which caught the words a little more strongly.

He said, "Well, it's got to be one of them, I guess."

Meshack was breathing hard, and so was I. We were both bleeding, too, and the scratch on his chest looked bad, but it was caking and clotting, and I hoped it was a good sign. I was still smearing blood every place I laid my hand, and the dull, dismal ache of the pain there felt as if it would eat my whole arm if it were left to rage unchecked.

He said, "I didn't even hear any screaming."

"Neither did I." But of course, I wouldn't have. I had to watch his mouth to catch all his words. "But you know what this means—it means they aren't just behind us. They're ahead of us, too."

"Ahead of us. Beside us. Behind us." He grimly ticked off the possibilities.

"Don't do that," I begged. "Don't. We'll find a way out. You said it yourself, out—or into a defensive position."

"And you said 'up.' Up isn't getting us very far. It didn't get *him* anywhere."

"It's getting us *up*," I argued.

Ahead there was noise of a scuffle and then sounds like whimpering—but we didn't hear any snapping beaks or cawing whistles except behind us, so we kept on going. How much farther could it be, anyway? How much farther could we go before we ran out of room to retreat?

Before long the way opened, and there was a pit down before us.

The pit wasn't deep, but it was wide, and it was full. And down in the thick of it, stood Nicodemus—thrashing and throwing things around. My lantern-light waned, and I set it down carefully before it went out all together.

"Meshack, give me your candles if you have them."

He reached into his satchel and pulled out a pair of fat, home-dipped tapers. I fought to light them from the last bits of the lantern's failing spark. While I cursed at the reluctant wicks, I tried to ignore Nicodemus and his sputtering, ranting mumble.

"Where is he? The rest of him, it's in here somewhere. The rest of lots of them, look at them, how long these have been here. Well, he's new. He'll be wet. They couldn't have just swallowed it, all of him, not in that nick of time when they took him and he was gone."

"Your pa's dead, Nick," Meshack said. There wasn't any unkindness in his words, but he said them firmly. "You left him down in the tunnel."

"He was right behind me!" our cousin hollered so that even I could hear him without struggling to understand. "And I went back! I went back when I noticed he weren't breathing and crawling behind me! You know what I found?"

Meshack told him, "I know what you found. We found it too."

"Why don't you look at what *I* found?" He asked it like an invitation. He asked it with a little bit of pride, and a little bit of madness. It wasn't a question. It was a declaration of insanity.

Just then, the candle wicks caught and our light promptly doubled, then tripled as I urged the second wick into flame. "Nicodemus," I said, "Your lantern's failing. Give me your pack, I'll light your candles..."

I don't think I managed to chew the whole word out.

As I was speaking, our light lifted up the shadows and I saw what Nicodemus was doing. I saw what he was throwing, and what he was digging his arms down into, lifting up pieces of detritus from the pit and throwing them left and right, over his head, behind himself.

"Jesus *Christ*," Meshack said.

I almost repeated the sentiment, not from blasphemous faith—but from pure astonishment.

The pit was filled with bones, and it was bigger than I'd thought.

There was no way to know how deep it went. There was no way to guess how many sets of mortal remains had been abandoned there. From a spontaneous accounting of the rounder domes, the skulls, I thought perhaps hundreds. I saw longer skulls too, more jagged shapes to the bones, and knew that the pit held more than men, but deer too—and dogs, and bears, and the spirits only knew what else.

"Get him out of there," I said, too horrified by the sight to move.

"*You* get him out," Meshack flapped his arm in his cousin's general direction. "I'm not going to make him do *shit*."

He leaned forward and rested that way, with his hands braced on his thighs.

"Nicodemus, get out of there," I ordered. I was so tired there wasn't much force behind it, and I didn't think he'd obey me, anyway. But I tried it again, and I handed Meshack a candle.

I walked over to the edge closest to my Mander cousin and held out my less-injured hand. "Take it," I told him. "Take it, and we'll get out of here."

"How?" He shrieked it at me, so loud I heard it with both ears—and it felt like a knife in my teeth.

I lifted my candle above my head in order to cast every bit of light it could. The chamber was honeycombed with passages that emptied into this very place. The ceiling was so tall that my light wouldn't reach it; I didn't know where the shadows ended and the cave began again.

"Boone?" I pleaded under my breath.

"Is that what you're doing?" Meshack asked without lifting his head. "Praying to the ghost of Daniel Boone? Don't tell me you're as crazy as everybody said. Please, uncle. Don't make me think that, not now."

"I'm not praying. I'm *asking*. It's not the same thing. And anyway, I saw him," I admitted, swinging my gaze from side to side, once again seeking help or shelter. "I saw him, and he's been trying to help us."

"Why?" And now there was the edge of mania in Meshack's voice too, and maybe it was in my own as well, but I could hardly hear my own words. "If he really wanted to help us, he would've told us to never come inside!"

"And would that have worked?" I was shouting now, too, because what was the point in keeping quiet? "Would we have stayed out—would *you* have stayed out if I'd told you, 'A ghost said we should leave it be?' You wouldn't have done it. *They* wouldn't have done it," I gestured at Nicodemus, who was dragging himself up and out of the bone pit, wading towards my outstretched hand.

And then Nicodemus asked a most startling question. In a casual voice, as if nothing odd or terrible were transpiring all around him, and as if he were not standing in a pile of bones as if it were a rain puddle, he said, "Who's that woman?"

Meshack didn't even look up to see. "There ain't no woman, Nick."

The Mander nodded hard. "Yeah there is. She talking to you." He pointed up and out, and his eyes were wide with astonishment, freshly big with a new kind of fear.

It amazed me, how the Mander had seen her first. It made no sense at all; he knew nothing of the spirits. But once she'd been duly indicated, I don't know how I could've missed her.

Meshack froze, and it looked to me as if he were waiting to be beheaded. He leaned forward, the candle clenched in his one hand and Nicodemus's gun in the other. He fixed his eyes on the slippery floor between his boots.

She crouched beside him and whispered at his ear. She placed her hand on his knee, beside his own hand, and she was chattering words, quickly, lightly.

I couldn't hear them.

Something about the way the light hit her told me that she wasn't there in any mortal sense. It was the way the flame licked through her; it was the too-smooth skin that had no pores, no eyebrows, and no fine lashes.

She looked like a large, coiled infant from some other species, wet and freshly hatched from an egg.

"Meshack?" I whimpered it like a child, because the phantom terrified me.

She wasn't like the flickering ghost of Boone, who came and went and looked mostly like an echo of a man. She was something else, or something worse—something weirder. She had no hair and she wore a gray dress that ended ragged at her knees, and her toes curled to catch the bumpy skin of the cave floor. She was barefoot, and bare faced, and bare headed.

Meshack wagged his head slowly back and forth, and he mouthed a response I couldn't catch. He still hadn't raised his eyes to look at her.

Whatever he said, she argued with it, and the fluttering consonants of their strained conversation told me nothing. When he shook his head, I think he said, "No, baby." And then he said something else, and I heard enough of its edges to infer the rest. "Not me alone. He comes too, or I can't go."

She scowled, and the shape of her face was so thoroughly insane that it may as well have been evil.

Won't.

And he said, "Then I won't go. Not without him."

She glowered at me and it was a hateful look that sucked all the breath out of my chest. I honestly feared that she would approach me, then; and the thought of it was enough to make my eyes water. I tried to retreat, though there was nowhere to go except into the pit with Nicodemus, and what kind of improvement would that be? So I held my ground and prayed to all the spirits who had ever shown me any kindness that please, please, *please*. Don't let that terrible phantom touch me.

She watched my terror with disinterest and disdain, wasting time and saying nothing until she came to some conclusion that I'd never understand. Again she pushed her face down close to Meshack's.

I believe she said, *Now or never, leave and stay gone.*

"What about you?" he asked, either tears or sweat moistening the whole of his face. "Whatever came of you? And why would you stay?"

She ignored the first question, but to the second she replied with a sing-song lilt, *This fray, it well becomes me.*

The phantom produced something in her hand; I don't know where she'd kept it hidden, or if I simply hadn't spotted it before. It was a flap of papers, and it was folded and laced shut. She passed the papers to Meshack and he finally tried to see her there, in that parting moment. But he winced and turned away.

Nicodemus stayed mired in the bone pit. He was afraid of the strange woman in that vague, dream-state way that didn't bother to process the reasons for his fright; but he was afraid of the bird things in a concrete, miserable way that inspired him to true terror.

And they were coming, creeping up fast and loud. By then my ears had recovered enough that I could hear it like a hum. My hearing was returning, but slowly. I faintly prayed, in case I had not yet exhausted my spiritual favors, that it might not be altogether destroyed after all.

The phantom woman leaned down again to say something more, and Meshack cringed away. She raised a hand as if to strike him, and stopped. She looked to me again and crooked her neck to indicate a hole beside me, and behind me.

I turned to see it, and against the raw, damp skin of my cheek there was air—I was almost certain of it. It was *moving* air that didn't stink so wholly of shit and decay.

"Meshack!" I said. "This way, it might be...it must be..." I floundered in my excitement.

Meshack was alone again. Nicodemus was at the edge of the pit, shaking and retching where he stood. It was odd to watch a man vomit that way, without crunching over or aiming his mouth at the ground.

"Get him," Meshack said. "And let's go." My poor nephew, he was shaking so hard, and dribbling blood down his forearms and chest. It was pooling against his belt, soaking his shirt. He'd be no help in lifting the other man out.

I tried to climb down gingerly, but I tripped and went face-first into the bone pit, bruising myself in ways too horrible to contemplate.

I staggered, and thigh-deep in the terrible wreckage of humanity I seized Nicodemus by the arm and dragged him—vomit and all—up over the edge and onto firmer turf.

"I thought you were going to leave him," I said to Meshack as I hauled the other man up. It was almost like towing a drowned man.

"We're going to need him."

"We are?"

"Yes, unless you want to stay here and live in the valley. And you don't want that anymore than I do. So it's got to be *him*." Meshack was staring down at the outermost paper, holding his candle past it and over it.

I'd forgotten he could read.

XVI.

The Instructions

Neither Heaster Wharton Senior nor Junior could read. The message must've been dictated.

First man out alive, Mander or Coy, whoever's got these papers gets the whole of my property on two conditions: One, he blows up the entrance to that cave our folks call the Witch's Pit and he leaves it closed forever. Two, he stays in the valley and sees to it that the cave stays shut.

My pappy and Mr. Boone, they should've killed that thing off when it was just the one. Maybe they didn't mean to let it live and breed. Maybe they didn't know it was full with a litter of little things, down there in the cave. Maybe they didn't know they'd only crippled it and made it madder, and meaner—and they'd let it birth some company.

Or maybe they were just scared and didn't know what else to do. I don't know. I weren't there. My pappy told me about it, though, and he told me he didn't think it was finished.

Well I know *it wasn't finished. And if my kin can't cut it off, then they'll have to live here with it. I know everyone wants me to divvy up the land all fair, so that's just as fair as I can make it.*

And if no one gets out, and no one ever reads this, it just goes to show that none of them deserved it anyway.